MISTY HORIZONS

SWATI JOSHI PHATAK

BLUEROSE PUBLISHERS
India | U.K.

Copyright © Swati Joshi Phatak 2025

All rights reserved by author. No part of this publication may be reproduced, stored in a retrieval system or transmitted in any form or by any means, electronic, mechanical, photocopying, recording or otherwise, without the prior permission of the author. Although every precaution has been taken to verify the accuracy of the information contained herein, the publisher assumes no responsibility for any errors or omissions. No liability is assumed for damages that may result from the use of information contained within.

BlueRose Publishers takes no responsibility for any damages, losses, or liabilities that may arise from the use or misuse of the information, products, or services provided in this publication.

For permissions requests or inquiries regarding this publication,
please contact:

BLUEROSE PUBLISHERS
www.BlueRoseONE.com
info@bluerosepublishers.com
+91 8882 898 898
+4407342408967

ISBN: 978-93-7018-958-4

Cover Design: Swati Joshi Phatak
Typesetting: Sagar
Illustrations: Manish Mehra

First Edition: March 2025

To those who walk a different path ...

Dedicated to Readers

I am grateful to,
Artist Manish Mehra who graciously
accepted to do the illustrations
and presented a visual window to my stories.

My heartfelt thanks to,
My parents, Pratima Joshi and Avinash Joshi for their blessings.
My husband, Vivek for all the support and encouragement.
My son, Surya for the inspiration.

Preface

Stories of 'Misty Horizons' were echoing in my heart for more than a year. And when I decided to write, the choice of language tilted towards English. There is a reason for that, and a beautiful one. 'Aanaya', my book of short stories was published in Hindi. It was appreciated by its readers across all the age groups from twenties to eighties.

However, I also got the feedback that stories could not reach to many readers, who were not well conversant with Hindi.

My desire to make my stories reach the wider spectrum of the readers, led 'Misty Horizons' to be in its present form. There are stories for everyone, because once again it is about emotions, hidden here and there in our day-to-day life. It is also about young people who are struggling to create their own ways of living in the backdrop of old social norms. It is also about people, who believe in their choices and make their own path even if they have to walk alone. Emotions are Universal, they are felt by all. Language is a medium, for emotions to travel through the words, when a story is told. And when it is read in the language you understand well, emotions are truly felt.

I present you, the stories of 'Misty Horizons' and hope you enjoy reading these.

Swati Joshi Phatak

Contents

1. Solo Trip 1
2. Coffee Cups 21
3. Interlude 29
4. Salon 49
5. Nuptial Bond 61
6. Heirloom 79
7. Reunion 95
8. Whirlpool 109
9. Inheritance 123

Solo Trip

"Solo trip? …. Why are you calling it a solo, when you are going in a group tour?" Vansh asked Ria.

"I need a break. Also, I do not want to bother myself with visa and itinerary planning." Ria took a sip of wine and looked at her friends, hoping someone to be in agreement with her. Vansh squinted his eyes, with a questioning frown and a puzzled look. He then asked Nupur, who was sitting next to him, "Are you also planning to go somewhere? Now a days solo trips seem to be a trend, especially among women."

"Yes, why not? I too will plan one soon." Nupur picked up a finger snack and put it in her mouth.

She then took a sip of her drink and said, "Vansh, women need a break from their families, hence they go on a solo-trip."

"I see…" Vansh said. He then asked Ria, "Who do you need a break from?"

"I need a break from myself…and …" she said something, but the music was so loud that nobody at their table could hear her. Vansh touched his ear and signalled Ria, that he could hear nothing. Ria, Vansh, Nupur and other common friends were at one of the roof-top restaurants of the city, to attend the ring ceremony of their friend. Guests were being called upon the dance floor. Middle-aged couples from the families of the would-be bride and groom had already reached the floor.

"And what, Ria?" Vansh bent forward on the table to listen to what Ria was saying, covering his one ear. Just then the music stopped and the mic was picked up by the brother of the groom, but before he could say anything, a voice echoed,

"And these stupid marriages …." Ria had replied loudly, so that Vansh could hear.

All the guests turned around and stared at their table. Ria was stunned and so were her friends at the table. There was an awkward silence for a moment, but groom's brother, who was holding the mic, laughed and said,

"You are right, Madam … I agree …marriage is a stupidity that we all love to do ….at least once ……" he winked at the groom.

"Well said, bro!!" Vansh raised his glass and said, "Cheers to marriage!"

Everybody at the table cheered and clapped. Vansh, Ria and Nupur along with other friends quickly walked towards the dance floor.

After a while, Ria left the dance floor. She was still feeling awkward for creating an embarrassing moment for her friend, who was getting married. She walked out of the banquet hall, came on the terrace and stood near the glass panels, installed before the parapet. She could see the vast expansion of the city, with twinkling lights of the high-rise buildings. Ria gazed at the moving vehicles, trailing the streams of light on the streets below.

Mood on the dance floor had changed. Couples were now swaying on the soft music. Singles had slowly moved away to the bar or to their tables. Mellow music made Ria feel good. She saw Vansh walking towards her.

"City never sleeps, right?" said Ria.

Vansh glanced at the street below and replied, "That phrase is more applicable for Mumbai."

"Hmm …" Ria nodded.

"So, running away from another alliance that your parents are suggesting?" He asked.

"Yes, true." Ria said, "Also, to answer your question, how my trip is solo, is that, no one, who I know, is going with me. Nobody will share my room. And nobody will tag along, when I just want to wander." She shrugged her shoulder and exhaled.

"Vansh, you are born and brought up in Mumbai, you won't understand the mentality of small-town parents."

"Not necessary." Vansh said.

Ria looked at him with a question in her eyes.

"I mean, people in a Metro city also could be conservative. I understand why are you disturbed but why are you focussing on running away from the situation you don't want to be in? Instead, work towards what you want." Vansh spoke with a concern.

"Let's see what happens after my trip. Maybe I would know what I want. I am thirty-two now, and still in a quest." Ria said and chuckled.

"What about Aditya?" Vansh asked.

"What about him?" Ria asked and walked back towards the hall.

-::-

Ria's parents were very happy when she had secured admission in one of the top colleges. They were thrilled when Ria was selected by one of the top global companies during the campus placement. Ria was ambitious and worked very hard. Her parents had proudly celebrated her promotions that came her way very fast, but when she crossed twenty-seven years of age, her parents started thinking about her marriage. Initially they coaxed her to get married but eventually they started pressurising her.

"You don't understand, Papa … my aspirations are different from what your generation thinks about life." She would try to explain her father. He would get anxious seeing the children of his friends and colleagues, getting married.

"What else you aspire to be? You are earning, living alone. That is more than enough." Her father would get annoyed.

"We are not going to get you married, just anywhere, Ria. We also know, you now earn, live independently. We will look for a suitable alliance for you." Her mother would explain her with care and mostly felt little under-confident herself. She was not sure if people had really changed their expectations from a girl.

"Ria, I do not know any other way of living happily, for a woman; if not married." Sometimes she would say helplessly.

"How happy didi is? Tell me." Ria had seen her elder sister getting exhausted managing job, children, home and her family after her marriage.

"Why? She is earning money, has two lovely children, her in-laws are happy. What else do you want? I do not understand what you girls look for?" Her mother would get frustrated.

On her parents' insistence, Ria had agreed to meet some of the alliances but no one could challenge her at intellectual level.

-::-

"Yaar, you are getting such rich alliances; I would say a yes instantly." Once her school friend Ankita had said jokingly.

"I will suggest your name then." Ria had said.

"Please do, dear. I want to get married in a family with generational wealth and lead a comfortable life. I will rear my children and enjoy my life." She was very clear. Ria often wondered as Ankita had studied with her and had got a good job but she was not interested in her career.

"You are so clear with what you want but don't you have any fear of losing your freedom?" Ria had asked her.

"I think, such families have a system in place. I will follow that." Ankita shrugged her shoulders and said, "Ria, I know that with my own capacities, I can never be that rich. I want to be part of a grand establishment that my future husband will inherit. So, I will do whatever is expected out of me, Period."

Ria was not surprised as she had seen many girls getting married into big families and adapting to the roles that they had previously opposed as part of the patriarchal system. Ria sometimes felt envious of her friends as they did not have any confusion regarding marriage. But she shuddered at the thought of getting tied down to a system.

"You are prejudiced, Ria. If the boy is good, isn't he being from a wealthy and well-established family a nice thing?" Ankita had once questioned.

"Losing your identity to the system won't bother you, Ankita?"

"Yes, I am fine by that, what is wrong? Aren't you a part of a corporate system?" Ankita had questioned her in a defensive tone.

"Not my whole life and not for twenty-four hours. I am growing and I am free! How can you compare these two?" Ria had argued but Ankita did not agree.

Eventually Ankita got married. After a few months she had invited Ria to her house for a function. Ankita was clad in an expensive saree and jewelry. She was moving around in the lawns of the huge bungalow of her in-laws. She was commanding the staff of the house, with an authority that she had acquired after her marriage. Ankita was taking the approval of her mother-in-law, for everything. And her mother-in-law seemed to be very proud of her. Ankita looked happy too, glowing with pride.

Ria tried to imagine herself in such house with a big family, with umpteen facilities and luxuries. But she could sense that, there was a well-defined chain of command to be followed. There was seldom any scope for individuality.

'It is so claustrophobic…. may be, one day, Ankita would be at the top of the pyramid in this system.' Ria thought and saw, Ankita was meeting and talking to everyone, who was invited. Alongside her husband, with a smiling face, she was making sure, that the guests were being looked after well. Ria was impressed.

'May be that is what Ankita really wants. It is just not me.' Ria thought.

She took a sip of coffee while watching Ankita. She felt, her friend had slipped in to a different league. Ria could not relate with her anymore. Eventually Ankita got busy in her married life and Ria joined another big firm while climbing the corporate ladder.

-::-

"But should everyone live in the same way, fitting into one sole system?" Once Ria had an argument with her mother, who had become very anxious after learning about Ria's friend, Ankita's marriage.

"I do not know any other way of leading the life or any other system." Her mother had said placing her tea cup on the table with a force.

"So, lets invent one." Ria had said in exasperation.

"What do you want? Disposable relationships? As and when required?" Her mother had retorted.

Ria had grown tired of having such arguments with her parents, every time she visited them in last few years. After one such argument, she had decided to go on a trip abroad.

-::-

Ria boarded the plane for her solo trip to Europe. She took her window seat and that was the time when she thought of Aditya, 'Adi' for her. She had avoided talking about him with Vansh on the rooftop restaurant. Ria had met Aditya at a Sufi music concert, named 'Kabira', in Delhi. She had found him very different from the men his age. He was very calm, composed and comfortable in his own skin. A clean shaven tall young man with thick mustache. Aditya gave a serious and thoughtful look until he spoke and laughed. They had got along very well. Ria was in the final year of her masters, after working for five years. Aditya was very sure of what he wanted in his life. He loved to travel, read the books, was deeply interested in history and was quite philosophical, still very practical. Ria felt very comfortable in his company. He was a patient and attentive listener.

Their friendship had started growing into something more but Ria was apprehensive. She was not ready for a relationship. She had finished her Masters and had joined a global enterprise that had offered her a very good position. Aditya had hinted towards a commitment and that had made Ria uncomfortable. Ria and Aditya had mutually parted ways. He was no longer part of her life. There was no bitterness as no promises were made.

-::-

Ria was thrilled when she looked at the screen in front of her. It was showing the image of the plane crossing the international border of India. 'Gosh! It feels surreal…,' she thought. Ria felt good, as the baggage of emotional pressure by her parents, was left behind.

A few hours later, it was very quiet in the plane, as most of the passengers had slept. Ria woke up to the announcement by the captain. His happy voice and the active cabin crew preparing the aircraft for landing, made Ria nervous and excited at the same time. She pulled the window shade up and felt happy to see the deep blue and grey clouds descending over the lush green pastures below.

The plane landed in Vienna. The tour guide, whose name was Jojo, was standing at the exit gate to receive all the travelers of the group. When they boarded the bus. Ria noticed, all of them were with their families, except for her.

'Don't they get bored always being together?' She thought.

The bus reached Bratislava. On Jojo's recommendation, Ria decided to take a walk in the old town of Bratislava, that was right behind their hotel. Some tourists ventured out in the alleys of the old town. Ria was walking on the cobbled streets. A dream that she had never shared with anyone but had nurtured since her teenage. She heard the giggles of the newlyweds in the tour group, who would sneak a moment to kiss each other. She smiled and kept walking. She reached the old town square, surrounded by old buildings and a fountain in the center. She looked around and twirled, spreading her arms.

After a couple of days in Slovakia, the tour headed to Budapest, where Ria enjoyed the cruise on river Danube, but did not like the families shouting, cracking jokes, laughing loudly. People were distributing snacks and sweets. She went on upper deck with her glass of champagne that was served on the cruise, and absorbed the beauty of the city, on both sides of the river, quietly.

In Prague, after the palace tour, the group was given some free time for a few hours. Ria was happy, she loved to wander alone. She saw tourists gathering around the astronomical clock tower at the old town square.

'Aah, that hourly show! Might as well, I see this.' Ria thought and walked towards the tower. It was getting cold. She wrapped her muffler around her neck and pulled her dark brown wavy hair out. She then tucked her hands in the pockets of her jacket and joined the crowd. As the hour struck, the puppets came out of the tiny window of the clock. People cheered. Ria was still standing there, waiting for the crowd to disburse.

"So much so for a few seconds of amusement. But there is an interesting story behind it." A familiar voice with a heavy baritone came over her shoulder.

'Adi ???' Ria wondered. 'No way!! how can this be possible?' She thought and turned around. To her surprise, she saw a tall young man with a beard, smiling at her.

"Hey, Ria, ..." the man smiled at her.

She kept looking at him. He was Aditya, her Adi. A man with a beard, in an off-white pullover, with a long tan jacket over it. Ria loved his look, as with a beret on his head and a Burberry muffler hanging lose around his neck, he gave an impression of a British writer from sixties. He was smiling at her.

"It's me, Adi …" he waved and said.

Ria felt little embarrassed, "Oh, yes … Hi Adi! …I just could not believe …. I mean, how?" She smiled then pointed at his beard.

"Yeah …. This." Aditya pointed at his face and laughed gently.

Ria smiled at Aditya and then she looked around him.

"Still single," said Adi with a smile.

'Gosh! how he reads my mind ….' Ria felt a little embarrassed but she was relieved to know his single status.

"You are with your family or someone?" Adi asked.

"No, no … I am alone … I mean with a group tour …but alone." Ria said making quick gestures with her hand.

"Aaah … get it. So, …would you like to take a walk?" Aditya asked, with one hand in his pocket and gesturing towards the old town square with the other hand.

"Sure", Ria said and tucked her hair behind her ears. She put her hands in the pockets of her jacket. When they were out of crowded area, Ria asked, "Adi, are you not surprised to see me here?"

"Hmm … No. I mean, one can go for a trip. Isn't it? Are you … surprised?" Aditya looked at her with a gentle smile and asked.

"Hmm …Probably not …" Ria smiled and replied thoughtfully.

"Yes, people travel. I am happy to see you, though." He did not hide it.

'Me too.' Ria wanted to say but she did not. She looked at him and smiled.

Aditya and Ria looked at the expanse of the old town square, soaked in yellow light. The open area was surrounded by beautiful old buildings with open café in the front. Ria remembered; Jojo had asked everyone in the group to assemble at the other end of the Charles bridge at ten pm.

Ria was contemplating what to do, just then Adi asked, "Coffee?" She immediately agreed and they both walked towards one of the street cafés, walking past an art gallery.

Aditya pointed at the gallery and said, "Works of Dali and Warhol are displayed there."

"Oh, okay." Ria smiled and nodded.

Aditya saw an empty table at a café and they both sat there. They ordered coffee and hot croissants. Aditya noticed, Ria had colored her hair brown and looked more mature than the time when they were together. He being tall, had to push his chair back to sit comfortably. He looked at Ria, who first removed her sling bag to hang on the chair and then realized that it had her passport; so, she put the bag across her shoulder again.

Aditya smiled knowing why she did so. His love for her had rekindled.

"So, you are with a group, but alone… I mean you are not with family or friends like others …. how has been the experience so far?" Aditya asked.

"Hmm… yes. … it has been good. How about you?" Ria, who loved Aditya's heavy voice, was on guard in her conversation, contrast to her inner feelings.

Aditya told he was on one of his usual solo trips and was exploring the place all by himself. He had read a lot thus learned about the place and its history.

"You enjoy it more when you know beyond what meets the eyes." Aditya said and moved backwards as the waitress got their coffee and croissants.

"So, you are actually traveling solo." Ria kept her arms on the table with her fingers intertwined.

"Yes, you can say that." Aditya bent towards the table to pick up his cup of coffee. He took a sip and looked at her. Ria got a whiff of his warm woody cologne. She liked it and felt good. She looked around and avoided looking into his eyes.

"I usually take a break twice a year, one to explore India and one to travel abroad." He kept his cup down and placed his elbows on table. Ria felt intoxicated with his perfume. She was trying very hard to concentrate on what he was speaking. Their conversation moved from their respective careers, politics, music to family and marriage. Ria told him in detail, about her parents pressurizing her to get married and how that had caused a distance between her and them. Aditya was listening to her intently.

"I just don't see myself as married, what about you?" Ria asked.

"I don't know as of now. But I like the idea of a stable family." Aditya looked thoughtful and was quiet for a moment, then he said, "As you know, my parents had separated when I was a kid, so, I value having my own family. A family where we support and celebrate each other's growth."

Ria understood what he meant. Aditya's parents had separated, when he was twelve-year-old. Both his parents were software engineers and his mother had surpassed his father in terms of growth in their career. She had bagged overseas projects and that did not go well with his father. He forced her to quit or let the promotions go. After a lot of mental harassment, Aditya's mother had ultimately filed for the divorce. She had handled her career and had raised Aditya on her own.

"My mother has retired and lives alone in Bangalore. She is now dedicated to social service. My father remarried though." Aditya said and took a sip of coffee.

Ria kept looking at him.

"Hey, I am hungry, would you like to eat something?" Aditya asked her.

"Pasta... maybe." Ria was at ease now but her heart skipped a beat, every time she looked into Aditya's brown eyes.

Aditya spoke about his plans to start a company where he could tell people about the history of the place by taking them for Heritage walks.

"You will quit such a fantastic job?" Ria was surprised. She instantly regretted for being judgmental.

"That is what one has to do, to start something new. Right?" Aditya smiled and looked at her.

"Of course ...are we going to meet again?" Ria asked in a happy tone.

"Why not? Unless, you don't want to." Aditya said jokingly.

Ria chuckled and asked him to wait while she went inside the café. She came out with a bag. Aditya offered to walk her across the Charles bridge, where Ria's bus was waiting. She agreed and felt good walking alongside him. Their hands brushed while walking.

Ria saw many fellow travelers walking back while few were still enjoying the view on the Charles bridge. Ria moved near the edge of the bridge to see the twinkling reflections on the water of river Vltava. Few couples were standing quietly, holding each other close. A few couples were kissing each other lovingly while talking. The sky with deep blue and slight orange hues had loomed over the bridge and over the span of the river and the beautiful buildings on its banks.

Aditya stood next to Ria, looking around. He turned towards Ria and was about to tell her something pointing at a building across the river when Ria raised on her feet and kissed on his cheeks. It was so spontaneous that Ria could not believe what she just did. Ria's lips touched the stubble on his cheeks and she felt the warmth of the fragrance that he wore. Aditya was taken aback and did not know how to react for a moment.

He looked at Ria, and his feelings were rekindled. He held her hands and bent to gently kiss on her forehead.

"I ... I don't know why I did that, Adi ..." Ria looked at him.

Aditya smiled and tucked her hair behind her ears, that were covering her face because of the wind and said, "Feeling is mutual."

Ria smiled, absorbing the words what Aditya had just spoken, while her heart was beating fast. They both smiled and then laughed, trying to ease what had just happened. They looked at each other, then Aditya bent over her face and gently planted a kiss on her lips. Ria shut her eyes and felt a wave traveling down her body. She had not been kissed before the way Aditya was gently kissing her. Ria felt loved and protected. She closed her eyes and responded kissing him back. It turned into a gentle lip lock for a moment, with his arms around her shoulder and waist. Ria felt melting in his arms.

They moved away from each other. Aditya looked into her eyes then rested against the parapet of the bridge, looking down at the river. Ria stood beside him. She was still taking in what had just happened. They both were quiet for some time, standing close to each other. They started walking across the bridge after a while, quietly.

"Wish you happy journey. Next time, try to include a train travel." Aditya said, after reaching near the bus, that was waiting for the members of the group.

"Will keep that in mind. Thank you. Wish you a great trip too." Ria wished him and handed him the bag that she had got from the café.

"Here, this is for you, a few pastries." She said.

"Wow, Thanks." Adi took the bag and waited until the bus left.

Ria was very happy and kept thinking about Aditya all the way while the bus reached the hotel. 'Am I ready for a relationship? For a commitment? Or I am reading too much into it? I like Adi, he is a sorted and truly a no-nonsense man. Doing well in his career, explorer by nature and has some dreams to do something different.'

She sat in the foyer of the hotel for a while and thought of what had happened on the bridge, 'Did that kiss mean anything? He did make me feel good. A good kisser? What am I thinking?' She smiled involuntarily. 'Was it only lust? But we did have a real conversation. I did feel close to him. His voice was so assuring. Am I secretly looking forward to a relationship? …..Oh my God!… No no, I don't want to settle ….' She exhaled, got up and walked towards the lift lobby of the hotel.

She could sense that she was not able to get over being with Aditya. The conversation, he walking along, wanting to tell her about the city, listening to her intently then their hands brushing and later he holding her firmly in his arms, for a few moments. This side of being woman had come alive for the first time.

Ankita had once asked her, "How come you never found any man? You are smart and attractive. Are you into girls?"

"No ..." Ria had retorted.

"You have reached thirty with no relationships? I will not let you reach forty like this. Will find someone for you." Ankita would say in a patronizing tone.

"Don't do that." Ria would tell her firmly.

-::-

Ria entered her hotel room and put her phone for charging. She removed her jacket, pulled her hair up and threw herself in the bed. A short while later she called Vansh and told him about meeting Aditya

"What? You met Adi there?" Vansh exclaimed.

"Yes ..." Ria smiled.

"Now, stay in touch with him.... at least as a friend. At last! I am happy for you, wishing you all the best!" Vansh said.

Ria took the shower, slipped in to an oversized sweatshirt and sweatpants, made a cup of coffee for herself. She took her phone and sat on the lounge chair next to the big glass window of her hotel room. She saw a message from Aditya, she smiled then looked outside the glass window. When she checked the phone again to go through the next day itinerary; a mail notification flashed. it was from her boss. She was thrilled to read that she was being given the charge of an independent project abroad. She immediately took her notebook and started typing her response to the mail. Ria's phone was now lying on the bed. A couple of messages from Aditya flashed on the screen of her phone.

-::-

Lawns of the hotel in Bangalore were beautifully decorated in a color theme of white. The guests were enjoying the conversation, while jazz music was playing in the background. Ria, who was in India for winter holidays, was talking with her friends, when everybody heard someone clink and raise the toast,

"Here for the couple made for each other. And for their newly launched company, 'Heritage Walk'. Wishing you both all the best for the new beginnings."

"To the new beginnings," everybody raised the toast and cheered.

"Hey … come for the group photograph." A friend called out, "Riaaa…."

"Coming …" said Ria and walked happily towards the gazebo, where Aditya and his beautiful bride were standing and smiling at each other; flanked with their friends.

Coffee Cups

Girish adjusted his flat cap, looked into the mirror, wrapped his muffler around his neck and wore his tweed jacket.

"Jayanti!!" He called out his wife, "I am ready."

He then approached towards the dining table. He looked at the cane basket that was kept on it. Jayanti had arranged everything that was to be kept in the basket, on the table. A box with a few slices of home-made ginger cake, another small box with a few cookies. Few tissues, one kitchen napkin, one water bottle and one coffee flask. Girish started placing the things in the basket.

"Girish, I am ready too." Jayanti emerged from the kitchen, carrying a tray with four small porcelain blue cups.

Girish smiled at her and picked up the cups from the tray to keep in the basket. Jayanti then put on her woollen cap, wore her jacket and shoes; while Girish checked the lights of all the rooms.

"So, how do I look?" Jayanti adjusted her hair and looked at her husband with a spark in her eyes and smile on her face.

"Great! as always." said Girish. They both walked towards the main door.

Every Sunday morning Jayanti and Girish, both in their sixties, would drive to Central Park. The park was densely populated with big trees and had a beautiful landscaping with a variety of palm trees, plants of different seasonal flowers and shrubs. Jayanti and Girish liked this park as it was designed for everyone with different needs. It had lush green lawns, jogging tracks, ponds, mounts, sitting areas, benches and small bridges across the ponds. There was proper parking and washrooms near every entry gate, for the visitors.

They both would take a walk for a short distance carrying their small basket of cane, with a coffee flask, four small cups, two books and something to eat. Their favourite place was a bench under a huge Gulmohar tree. They would sit on the bench, placing their cane-basket between them. They would read out a poem or a few lines to each other, from their favourite books. Girish would then pour hot coffee in the cups which they both would relish sitting on the green bench, watching people. They would often remember and talk about memorable moments and events in their journey of life so far.

It was a usual Sunday morning in the park. Jayanti and Girish were sipping coffee and reading their books. In between, Jayanti looked up and enjoyed watching people. She was curious to see a young girl around twenty, who had passed them a couple of times while jogging. The girl looked at her and smiled; Jayanti smiled back. She was tempted to talk to her but was not sure if she should, as she had experienced that people did not like to talk, interact or make friends unlike the times when she and Girish were young.

Jayanti finished reading a poem, placed her finger on the page and closed the book, to take another sip of coffee. She saw the same girl, who was jogging and had passed a smile at them. The girl was panting and coughing. She had slowed down and stopped almost in front of their bench. The girl bent down, as she had a bout of coughing. Jayanti placed her coffee cup on the bench, got up and walked towards her.

"What happened? Are you okay?" She lovingly asked the girl.

"Nothing .... just coughing .... pollens and dust-allergy,..." the girl answered while coughing.

"Why don't you come and sit on the bench?" Jayanti pointed towards the bench. Girish looked up from the book and saw Jayanti talking to the girl.

The girl first hesitated then agreed. She walked towards the bench, Girish promptly got up and moved the basket towards the corner of the bench. The girl sat and pulled out a small water bottle from the pocket of her jacket and drank some water. She was little breathless and was still coughing; little less though.

Jayanti asked the girl, "Would you like to have some hot coffee? You will feel better."

"No, Thanks Aunty... uh ...Madam.... I am fine." Girl replied wiping her watery eyes.

Jayanti smiled at the confusion of the girl and gestured for coffee, looking at Girish. He was standing at the other end of the bench, holding his cup of coffee. He kept his cup on the bench and promptly took out one blue porcelain cup from the basket and said,

"Why don't you join us for a cup of hot coffee, you will certainly feel better."

The girl looked at him and politely said, "I am good, Sir. Thank you."

Girish still poured some hot coffee in the blue cup and handed over to the girl. The aroma of the coffee spread in the air and the girl could not refuse the steaming cup of hot coffee. She took the cup of coffee from Girish and said, "Oh …Thank you, Sir."

The girl took a sip pf coffee and closed her eyes. She took a deep breath and exhaled, "It is good…"

Jayanti was happy to see the girl feeling better. She picked up her own cup, extended it to Girish, "Pour me some more."

"Here you go..." he said then he poured some coffee for himself too.

The young girl realised that Girish and Jayanti were still standing. She got up and requested them to sit. She then introduced herself as Chitra. She was studying masters in social science. Jayanti took out the boxes of cake and the cookies and offered her. Chitra picked up one piece and saw the books that Jayanti and Girish were reading. She told them that she too enjoyed reading books. Three of them had a conversation that none of them had ever imagined.

Jayanti wondered if some friendship had brewed among them. She was happy that she had never missed on keeping two extra cups for coffee. She always thought that may be someday, somebody would like to converse with them and the morning could have more laughter and more joy. That day she had returned home happy.

Jayanti and Girish were still going to the park. Their frequency had reduced though. Sometimes they met Chitra and they discussed and exchanged the books. Few years had passed by.

-::-

Jayanti was visiting the park after a long time. She was sitting on the bench with the cane basket next to her. A few more benches were installed making it a sitting arrangement in a square. Jayanti was holding a book but her eyes seemed like waiting for someone. She smiled as soon as she saw a young woman approaching her, carrying some books and a bag. Jayanti looked happy upon seeing her.

"Good morning, Chitra." Jayanti waved at her.

"Good morning, Jayanti!" Chitra bent and hugged Jayanti.

She then sat on another bench, next to Jayanti's and said, "Our book club is expanding! Mona and Divya are on their way."

Jayanti smiled and took out a book from her basket. She had insisted that Chitra called her by her first name, when she learned, that was the trend. Youngsters called their seniors by the first name.

Chitra took out some sandwiches from her bag and placed them on a plate. She then took out the flask and two blue porcelain cups from Jayanti's basket. She poured hot coffee in one cup and handed over to Jayanti. Jayanti took the cup and looked at the other corner of the bench where Girish used to sit. She looked up and smiled. Chitra's eyes welled up. She smiled and poured another cup for herself. They both lifted their coffee cups and looked up.

"To Girish…" Jayanti said with moist eyes.

"And to our friendship…" said Chitra and smiled.

They both looked at each other with a tender smile, and continued talking about the books they had brought, while sipping their hot coffee in the blue porcelain cups.

Interlude

Deepti was dreading the weekend. Akash was supposed to come back from Bangalore. It had been over a few months since she and Akash were trying to adjust with each other, but more they did, more things went wrong. She was driving back home from her office and for the first time she did not mind the traffic.

It was just two years back when Akash had moved-in with Deepti in her apartment. It was nearer to the offices of both of them. Akash and Deepti had met at a common friend's house-warming party and had got along well. After meeting a couple of times, they dated for almost a year and eventually declared their relationship to their respective parents. Both of them were in their early thirties and their parents had happily accepted their relationship status.

After having worked for a few years in India, Akash wanted to move back to the USA to work and study further. Deepti did not want to leave India.

"I do not believe in a long-distance relationship." Akash had declared at the end, when he quit his job.

"You please think over this. I am going to Bangalore to spend some time with my parents. Also, there is some paperwork to be done. It may take two to three weeks. You will get enough time to think." Akash had tried his best to convince her to move, if not immediately, maybe later.

"You can think too, Akash …." Deepti had urged, "Your parents are also here. You do your research and come back."

She had tried to convince him but she knew, he was not worried about his parents as his elder brother was there in Bangalore. Few weeks went by without any decision. Akash was to return on the weekend. Deepti's heart was getting heavier. She had not told her parents about Akash's future plans.

Deepti reached her township, parked her car at the parking in the basement and chose to take the stairs instead of elevator. Her cook had already reached and was cleaning the kitchen. She told her to make pasta and went to take bath.

Deepti took a long shower then soaked herself in the body cream. She wore her robe and stood near the room heater as she felt cold. She opened her wardrobe and reached out for her sweatshirt and trackpants. While pulling her clothes out, her black dress slipped out of the wardrobe and fell on the floor. She picked it up and held in her hands. Deepti caressed her soft black dress and thought of the time she had worn it last. She remembered the night she was wearing that dress.

-::-

Deepti and Akash were returning home from a party, and the topic of moving to the US had come up. They argued while

Akash was driving, until they parked their car in the basement. They were quiet in the elevator while it reached their floor. They both had walked towards their apartment controlling their anger. She had opened the lock and they both had entered without looking at each other.

Their argument had resumed, as soon as he had shut the door.

"You are very selfish, Akash." Deepti said feeling disappointed.

"You are calling me selfish? It is called being ambitious." Akash clarified.

"Oh, really?" Deepti's tone was sarcastic, but she was in pain.

"Are you not? Your promotion is due and this is your crucial year. You are working day and night for that. .... And come on, how can you call me selfish? Have I not adjusted for you? I moved in here, in your apartment from my pad, which is still lying vacant ...." Akash reacted while changing his clothes.

"What???" Deepti was stunned. "That was your convenience .... don't put it on me like you have obliged me.... your office is near from here .... are you not saving your time and spared from driving so long ....?" Deepti asked him in an angry tone.

"Yes, but I am sharing the expenses by fifty percent .... even our cars are used equally." Akash replied looking at her. He had changed into shorts and t-shirt. He hung his clothes on the hanger, put them in the wardrobe and walked out of the bedroom.

Deepti, who was still holding her sandals in her hands, threw them down on the floor. She was irritated by the comfort and the confidence that his body language reflected. She kept standing there for a moment. When she did not hear anything, she walked out of the bedroom and saw him sitting comfortably on the wing chair, browsing through his phone in the living room. Seeing him at ease, Deepti walked towards him fuming, breathing heavily in the state of anger.

Her hair fell lose on her bare shoulder. Deepti was wearing her black dress that was showing the tender skin of her shoulders. She walked towards Akash and bent over him grabbing his t-shirt by the neck.

"How dare you put me in this state then come and sit here as if nothing has happened …?" She looked straight into his eyes …. breathing heavily with anger.

He looked up at her but said nothing.

"Oh, yes …. you are now in your cave!!" She flung her arms in the air and said in a sarcastic tone.

Akash was not ready for this sudden outburst, though he was still upset but she had come so close to him, that he wrapped his arms around her waist as a natural reaction and looked at her. Deepti suddenly felt the loss of words. Akash held Deepti by her waist, while she was leaning on him. Her face was so close to his that they both ended up kissing passionately. They both went to the bedroom, made love and slept with exhaustion.

-:::-

Deepti felt sad seeing the dress.

'Was that our last love making? …. Is there any love left?' She wondered. She was feeling abandoned emotionally. She quickly kept the dress back on the hanger in the wardrobe. Akash's shirts were hanging next to her dress. She gently kissed one shirt and inhaled deeply to feel him near her. She changed into sweatshirt and trackpants then went to the dining room. Her dinner was ready. The cook had laid the table and had left already. Deepti had her dinner and went to sleep.

Next morning, she woke up to the sound of the doorbell. She opened the door and saw Akash standing outside. She smiled at him and suppressed her urge to hug him. He smiled back but it was formal. She felt the pain. He came and sat on the sofa. Deepti saw, there was no luggage with him. She understood, that he went first to his apartment to keep his luggage before coming to her.

Deepti felt a lump in her throat and felt choked after hearing whatever Akash had told her in one go, sitting across her wing chair. After a while he got up and took out his large suitcase from the cabinet in their bedroom and started dumping in whatever belonged to him. His shirts, jackets, shoes, books. He then went to the bathroom and took his belongings from there. He appeared to be doing everything in a jiffy.

Deepti could not witness it any longer, she went to the balcony of their bedroom and sat on the swing. Morning was still cold, she wore her jacket over the sweatshirt, she was ready to bear the chill rather than seeing her heart and her home being vacated.

Akash picked up the suitcase and placed it on the carpet of the living room as he knew that Deepti never liked suitcases being kept on the bed. He just sat there for a moment, with his head down staring at the floor. He felt torn but he had a lot of dreams to fulfil and for that he needed to move out of India. After his MS in the USA, he had thought that he would work in India forever but after a few years, he thought of going back to pursue research. He had gone to Bangalore to tell his parents about his decision and spend some time with them.

After landing at night, he had gone to his pad and had come to Deepti's apartment the next morning. When Deepti had opened the door, she had smiled with a flash of hope on her face, that is when Akash had asked her to sit on her wing chair and had told her that his decision was final. He had started working towards moving. In next three months, he would be at Princeton.

Deepti did not know how to respond; she had looked down and then looked up the ceiling. Her eyes had welled up. Her heart was sinking. She had got up, picked up her jacket and had walked away to sit in the balcony.

"Deepti …." Akash called her. He came in the balcony.

"Deepti …" He sat on the chair next to her, "I wish this had not happened; you are a wonderful person …. I wish you all the best."

She understood that it was time to say goodbye. For a moment she felt like running in to his arms. It was a fleeting moment …. Deepti did not look at him. She feared of showing her weakness. She looked away. Akash sat there for a while. He wanted to have a proper goodbye. A goodbye that would give him a closure. Probably it was too early for that.

Deepti's heart was pounding. She was somehow managing it. Akash took out the house key from his pocket and kept on the small table next to her. She wondered if he had those, why did he ring the bell in the morning?

"Good luck, Deepti." Akash said in a soft tone.

Deepti swallowed a lump in her throat but did not look at him.

"Cab has arrived." Akash checked his phone and spoke.

Deepti nodded. Her eyes were welled up.

Akash immediately got up. He feared, a minute longer would shake him. He went to the living room, picked up his bags and walked out; shutting the main door behind him.

Deepti was still in the balcony. She saw the cab entering the society campus and then parking in front of their tower. She saw Akash coming out of the building and sitting in the cab. Usually, that was the spot where Akash would look up and wave before sitting in the cab whenever he went out on the tours and next wave would be when the cab would turn from the main gate. She secretly hoped that he would look up. He did not.

There were no goodbye waves.

Akash had really gone.

Deepti kept sitting there on the chair with her knees near her chest. She looked at the tiny book shelf and the lamp on her left and at the chair next to the tiny wooden table on which the key was lying. Sound of the doorbell startled her. She got up and went in to open the door.

"Madam, you are not feeling well? What happened?" her cook enquired then went straight into the kitchen.

Deepti did not reply. She sat on the dinning chair. Looking at her tired face, cook made her some ginger tea. Deepti looked at the steaming cup of hot tea and smiled at her.

"Thank you, di …." She picked up her cup and then noticed, there were two cups.

Cook looked around and asked "Sir has not come yet?"

"No …." she said and the sense of realisation made her bitter. She got up and walked into her bedroom. Cook took the other cup in the kitchen.

Deepti was lost in her thoughts when the phone rang. It was her mother.

"Hello …. Deepti, I have a seminar to attend on Monday and the venue is near your office. So, I thought while returning I will stop by to have a cup of tea with you. Are you still working from home? It has been long since I met you and Akash." Her mother spoke enthusiastically.

Deepti's heart beats increased. She did not want to tell her parents about Akash and her breakup, that she herself was secretly hoping to be a temporary phase. She always took pride in her parents' belief in her. They had always supported her decisions. And her relationship with Akash was one of those. She wanted to keep them happy. She was silent for a while.

"Hello, beta …are you there? …Arre baba I am not going to ask you to get married." Her mother gently laughed.

"No, Mom…... actually…... Akash is on a tour for a month." Deepti replied.

"Not a big deal. I will spend some time with you, will meet Akash later." Her mother said.

"Yes, ok mom. …. you come. I will be home." Deepti answered.

Deepti was overwhelmed and disconnected the call as she did not want her trembling voice to give her away. Her mother was very practical and Deepti found it difficult to share her emotional side with her mom.

She spent the whole weekend mostly lying in the bed and tried to immerse herself in the work from home on Monday, but she could not continue for long and took off after half day. She thought of her mother's arrival in the evening and realised her mother can sense the void as many of Akash's things were not there. She found his old shaving items in the bathroom cabinet and a few colognes; she put them on the bathroom shelves. She hung Akash's old jacket on the pegs behind the door. She had yet to process the separation herself and had no strength left to deal with her parents; especially her mother.

-::-

"Mom, stay more." Deepti said while keeping the breakfast plates in the sink.

"No, beta. I will come again. I have already stayed overnight that was not planned." Her mother said, patting her cheek. "I have education seminar at Habitat Centre on Thursday; I have to prepare for that. Your Dad must be waiting too."

Deepti insisted and drove across Delhi in the morning to drop her mother.

"Deepti, have some tea." Her mother asked.

"No mom, I will get late for the office." She said and removed her office bag from the back seat and kept on the front seat then sat in her car, waved at her parents and drove to the office. She was still dealing with a sinking feeling. Her phone rang that was connected to the speakers of her car.

"Yes, I am on my way. You set up the meeting." She told the caller and disconnected. Deepti was constantly thinking about Akash and her differences with him, when she suddenly felt some discomfort and slight breathlessness. She felt her mind was fogging.

"Is it the pollution again?" Deepti wondered but soon her discomfort manifested as palpitation and she felt energy draining out of her body. Her face became pale and she experienced weightlessness. She felt shortness of breath. She slowed down and the drivers in the vehicles behind her started honking. She gathered some courage and slowly steered her car to the left and stopped by the side of the road in front of a building.

Deepti was shivering while sitting in her car. She was gasping for the breath; her palms were wet. She frantically looked for something in her office bag, she found few candies, she took one and fidgeted with the wrapper to open and kept the candy in her mouth. She drank some water with shaking hands. Just then the guard of the building knocked at her car window and told her to move the car from there. She looked at him, nodded and tried to move the key in the ignition with trembling hands. She slowly drove ahead and entered a nearby hospital. She felt very weak to steer the car but managed to park the car. She got out of the car and stood for a while; and later dragged herself towards the corridor of the hospital.

Deepti opened her eyes and found herself lying on the hospital bed. An attendant standing next to her bed assured her and called the doctor. ECG and a few blood tests were prescribed. Later in the Doctor's cabin, she gave Deepti some medicines and told her that she had experienced a panic attack.

"Don't take stress and don't overthink." Doctor smiled at her.

Deepti called up at the office and informed that she would be working from home for the next few days. She reached home and went to bed. She woke up when her cook came in the evening. She gave her tea and Deepti felt better but a strange sadness wrapped around her head. She thought of going to nearby market to buy some fruits. She told her cook, put on her jackets and loafers and went out. As soon as she entered the lift, she became anxious and felt weightlessness. When the doors of the lift opened on the next floor, she quickly came out and used the stairs to go down.

'Is it because of the weakness? Why are my legs shaking?' She thought.

Deepti walked out of the society gate; she heard the cars honking and she felt blinded by the headlights of the moving cars. Her feet froze. She was not able to move ahead. She quickly turned back and entered the society gate. Deepti felt that guard at the gate was laughing at her. She sat down on a bench near the gate. She felt palpitation and her palms were cold and sweating. She saw a few women staring and at her. She got up slowly and started walking back to her block, she felt scared.

-::-

A few days had passed. It was not new for Deepti's cook to see her being at work from home but she knew that Deepti loved to go to office every day and so did Akash.

Deepti had stopped going out altogether, after her repetitive experiences of fear as soon as she stepped out.

'Should I see a counsellor or should I talk about my break-up with my friends or Mom and Dad.' She often thought but she did not do either. It had been almost a month since Akash had gone and she had not yet come to the terms to her being single again. Deepti continued working from home. She either ordered things online or sent her cook or maid to the market. She stopped going to the salon and booked home service.

One evening she finished her office call and checked her mail. She was happy to see a good review from her boss about her work. She smiled and she felt it was probably for the first time she had felt happy from within, after Akash had gone. She thought of celebrating the good feedback.

Seeing Deepti smile, her cook asked, "Is Sir coming soon?"

"No" Deepti said. "You make ginger cinnamon tea; I will quickly get hot samosa from the sector market."

Immediately after saying this, she became uncomfortable. Cook was looking at her, she did not want to reveal her fear to the cook. She picked up her car keys, wore her jacket and stepped out. She felt nervous. She quickly got down using the stairs and reached her parking slot in the basement. Her mouth dried up and heart-beat increased and she felt scared by the time she reached to her car. She took a deep breath and opened the door, but could not sit in. She shut the car and looked around. She slowly walked towards the stairs and hastily climbed up all the fleets up to her floor and rang the doorbell of her flat.

Cook was surprised to see her sweating in winters.

"I forgot the purse." She said and sat on the sofa, with her head down trying to catch a breath. She felt safe upon reaching home.

"Didi, what should I make for dinner?" Deepti heard a voice coming from a distance. Deepti looked up, she saw her cook was standing with a cup of tea. Aroma of ginger and cinnamon made her feel good and safe. She picked up the cup of tea, told her what to cook and asked her to lock the door while leaving.

Deepti went to her bedroom, kept the cup on the side table and threw herself in the bed. She started crying. She stared through the sliding glass door of the balcony. The leaves of the plants kept out were swaying in the evening breeze.

"You are also stuck like me? In your pot. Isn't it?" She said and muffled her mouth with the blanket. She pulled up the blanket and wrapped her arms around her legs. She was awake sobbing till late in night with her head rested against the wall.

-::-

Deepti woke up as the sun rays through the glass doors fell on her face. She looked at the wall clock, it was 10 am. She checked the phone and sprang up seeing four missed calls from her father.

"Oh my God! How come I could not hear the ring?" She said to herself and quickly sat up to call her father.

"What happened? How she slipped? Why in ICU? I am so-so sorry, Dad. I am reaching, I am reaching, don't worry." She said in a panic.

"Are you okay? Mom should be fine. They will move her to the room once she regains consciousness." Her father replied in a tired voice.

"I am starting right away, Dad. Don't worry." Deepti said with concern.

"Don't come in a hurry. Things are quite under control now." Her father tried to calm her.

Deepti quickly got ready, packed her bag with few pairs of clothes, checked her purse for cards and money. She then picked up her car and house keys and walked towards the door and just then she was suddenly gripped by an unknown fear and felt low on energy. She felt a wave draining her energy down and was caught up with severe anxiety. She ate an apple and sat down on the couch as she started experiencing the palpitations. She removed her shoes and lay down on the sofa.

'Not again, God please…' she joined her hands and started crying.

'I am feeling so scared. … I don't want to.' Tears rolled down her cheeks. 'Should I go by a cab? But, I … I just can't get out of my house. How long it will be?' Her hands were shaking, while eating the apple which she could not finish, just then the phone rang. Her father was on a video call.

She immediately wiped her tears, picked up her phone, "Yes Dad …"

"Deepti … hope you have not left home yet. Mom is conscious now. They have moved her to the room from the ICU but she will be under observation. She is feeling weak but wants to talk to you."

Deepti brought a smile on her face and held the phone straight while, her hands were trembling.

"Deepti …. beta …come to me …" Her mother spoke in a feeble voice. She looked totally shaken.

Deepti with a heavy lump in her throat looked at her mother who suddenly looked very old to her.

"Yes Mom … I am coming …. coming right away."

"Come …quickly, I want to see you…." she raised her hand but her arm fell on the bed because of the weakness.

Deepti touched the screen and cried inconsolably.

"I am coming Mom …. we will have our ginger tea together, right?

Her mother nodded and smiled. Deepti disconnected the call.

She forced herself out and soon she was on the road amid heavy traffic. She continued driving in the middle of the road. She stopped at the red signal, and found herself surrounded by vehicles, she sensed getting a panic attack but told herself, 'It's alright, It's alright.' She saw the traffic light turning green but she froze. People in vehicles behind her started honking. "Yes…yes …" she mumbled and looked for her car keys. A flower selling boy knocked the window and pointed at the key which was already in the ignition slot.

"Oh, thank you." She looked at the boy with a gratitude.

She took a deep breath and slowly moved the car to the left of the road and put the blinkers on. She was exhausted. Her palms and feet were cold. She saw a banana cart on her left, she rolled the window down and bought some bananas. She started eating one. Just then a traffic policeman at a distance, waved at her to move the car.

"Madam, you cannot park here."

"Sir, I have only stopped for a while." She pleaded.

"No, you cannot stop here either." He said and looked at her. She looked perplexed.

"Madam, are you ok?" He asked with concern.

"I am fine, please give me a minute. Thank you, Sir." She said and rolled her window up. She then started driving and looked at the signboard at the next signal. She burst into crying and a laughter at the same time and exclaimed, "Oh, I am almost there!"

Deepti parked the car and rushed to the reception desk of the hospital. She enquired about her mother's room and climbed up all the stairs to the second floor. She saw her father carrying a coffee cup to the room. She hugged her father and apologised for not being contactable.

Deepti went near her mother's bed. Her mother smiled and held her hand. After a week, her mother was discharged from the hospital. She decided to stay for a week with her parents. One evening, her father made ginger tea and brought the tray in the living room. Her mother slowly walked in and sat on the sofa. Deepti put a soft blanket around her and then handed her the cup of tea.

Her mother smiled and said, "Aaha …ginger tea made by your dad … I am back home …." She then held Deepti's hand and said,

"Everything passes …. Isn't it?" She looked at Deepti with a smile.

Deepti held her hand and nodded. She suddenly realised that she had not thought of Akash for last few days.

"I will go home now, but I will come again to check." She told her parents.

"No, I am fine, you take care of yourself now. Akash also might be returning next week." Her mother said.

"Hmmm …" She said and hugged them both. She decided to tell them about her separation once her mother was perfectly fit and fine. Before leaving her parents' house, she went to her room and called Akash.

"Hello Deepti! …how are you?" Akash asked softly.

"Hey Akash …. I am good, I am good now …and will be better in coming times. …." She paused and said "But hey, I called you to say bye …."

"It …it is difficult for me too … and painful too…please know this." Akash spoke apologetically.

Deepti felt good.

"You know, but in the long run …." Akash continued.

"Akash, Wish you all the best." Deepti interrupted.

"Thank you…... all the best to you too Deepti, and Thank you so much for this call." Akash was sounding grateful.

"Bye, Akash." said Deepti and disconnected the call.

Deepti waved bye to her parents and left for her office from her parents' house. She kept driving calmly. After an hour she passed the building where she had got her first panic attack. The expressions on her face changed, she felt anxious again for a moment, but she continued driving. Her heartbeats got little faster but she smiled and shook her head. The feeling of anxiety faded away. She felt happy and liberated. She had got the closure. She changed the gear to speed up and her car became one of the cars on the Expressway.

Salon

A day before my sixtieth birthday, I treated myself with a long day of beauty treatment in my usual salon that had undergone an extensive renovation. Its new facade looked grand. New plush interiors created an ambience of a lounge with soft music that played in the background.

'When they can make the place look so good, I am sure they will renew my look too.' I smiled at my own thought and mentioned about my appointment at the reception. The receptionist confirmed and asked me to take a seat. When I was young, these places were called exactly what they did. Beauty parlour! Where we went with a hope and stepped out looking better versions of ourselves, or so we believed.

As a professor in the University, I seldom had the time for my vanity but since this salon was nearby, I could manage my maintenance. After my retirement, both my sons, in their mid and late twenties, had planned a birthday party for me in a hotel. They had roped in my husband for making a guest list. They thought it was a mile stone, and needed a celebration to mark the beginning of the second inning of my life. I was thrilled and I wanted to look my best.

"Madam, your skin is still so glowing, but it is slightly flaky, due to winters. Why don't you take our facial known for hydration, especially for working women like you. You will love it, madam," the girl who was threading my eyebrows, had stopped for a while, to check my skin and told me.

I enjoyed her marketing tactic, making women feel special, though I thought it was high time they changed it.

"Why, is it not for everyone?" I asked.

"No, madam, it works for all. But, working women have more stress." The girl replied sheepishly.

I relinquished my urge for correcting her and just said, "Hmm … ok, do my upper lip, then we will see." I shut my eyes, and prepared myself for the pain.

'So much so, to stop the masculinity showing on my face.' I thought, pressing the area above my upper lip, that had turned red; with my fingers.

"You are right though, …my skin has become dry …I do have my facial appointment." I examined my skin closely, while checking my eyebrows and upper lip and told the girl who was looking at me in the mirror.

"But I have not chosen yet. Which one should I go for? Ok, could you get me your catalogue please?" I asked the girl.

She promptly brought a glossy spiral bound book and gave it to me. I decided to take one of what she had recommended; not without checking the column at the right-side first.

"This one." I tapped on one name, from the list of facials.

"Sure Madam, perfect choice. ... Would you like to have some coffee or tea? She asked and requested me to sit in their lounge area.

"Coffee will do..." I said and walked towards their lounge area. I sank in a huge leather sofa as soon as I sat on it.

I could not control my own laughter and wondered, 'How will I get up?'

Soon a boy came with a tray carrying a steaming cup of coffee and a few cookies in a plate. He placed it on a coffee table in front of me. I felt happy, like a child. Anything unexpected and extra on the platter always made me happy. I took a sip and remembered what my friend, Payal, who according to the employees of this salon and probably by many people in the world; was not a working woman as she was a housewife. Even though she and many others like her were giving salons a huge business.

Payal always used to say, "You know, Chitra, whenever I feel depressed or low, I go to the salon."

"Hmm, you feel good, as you step out looking your best?" I had asked rather had tried to guess her theory.

"No, no, no Chitra, ..." she had quickly negated my guess.

"It is that absolute sense of validation! I love that. Whatever you tell them, the girls and the hair-dressers listen to you and make you feel good about yourself." She had an amazing smile on her face when she told me about her therapeutic discovery.

"Don't you think, it is for the money that you are paying?" I said and immediately regretted for having burst her feel-good factor. I felt small.

"I knew it." She feigned anger. "You emotionless professor, would certainly say something like that…. Listen, Chitra …you are paying say for a haircut, not for your talking. But they listen to you; your questions are so well answered. Ever heard them talking with each other? They don't trivialize anything. It is so … so relaxing." She almost had a faith in Salon.

My visits to the salon used to be short and quick. But it occurred to me that Payal was right. While sitting there and sipping my coffee, I felt that it was not just my skin, but my ego was being nourished too.

-::-

I took another sip, and picked up one cookie. Coffee was smelling good and cookies looked fresh. I took a bite and looked around. It was a beautifully done up lounge corner with panelled walls in Ebony on which huge mirrors and pictures were put up aesthetically. Most of the clients were young women and a few middle aged. I could see that each client was behaving like, it was her day. And they all looked happy.

There was a bride, who walked out like a princess in her beautiful gown. Then there was a woman in her forties seemingly struggling to cope with the changes in her body but walked out looking happy with beautiful wavy brown hair. Every woman was being pampered like a queen in the salon.

'Payal was right.' I thought.

I picked up one of the glossy magazines kept there. A woman came and sat next to me with her cup of coffee. I could smell an expensive perfume. Her hair dresser, who was a young man, came with a couple of huge glossy wire bound cardboards, with fake hair strands in various colours attached on those.

"Madam, that is amazing ….one should go for some change in life. Your hair texture is good, streaks of this colour will enhance the beauty and volume." Hair dresser said with a tone of approval and praise both.

He was a tall, well-groomed young man with a beard, who looked like a body builder too. And then it struck to me, it was not just their black uniform, but their beard made all the male hairdressers of the salon look alike.

"Make sure this looks good on me." The lady said with an authority but with a flirtatious smile.

"Madam, don't worry …. it will the look great." He got up, holding all the catalogues and then bent down again to show the shades.

"So, this shade is final? …." He asked the lady.

The lady nodded.

"Ok Madam, I will prepare the work-station."

"Work station!!" the lady raised her brows and said with a smirk.

Hair dresser slightly bowed, took the sample books and walked away. He went in a room at the end of the alley of salon-chairs and huge mirrors.

The lady looked at me, passed a smile and picked up one magazine. She did not seem much interested in reading the magazine. I was tempted to talk to her. I was wondering what could interest her, as she looked like someone straight from the web series "Bollywood Wives". She was wearing a pant suit and a huge silk scarf. Her hair was dark brown and she wore rings with big stones, on the fingers of both her hands. Her nails were beautifully done up. To me, she already looked so beautiful and ready that I wondered what else was left to be done. Her skin was spotless and she wore minimal makeup, but her eyes and lips looked beautiful. She was looking glamourous.

"Hi," I said.

She smiled and her phone rang just when she was about to respond. She gestured to be excused and took out her phone from her stylish big bag. It was a video call. She turned her back towards me but the screen of her phone was visible to me. I turned my face away and pretended to read my book but was tempted to see the screen of her phone. There was a smart middle-aged man with a salt and pepper crown on his head, talking on the screen. He seemed to be calling from a golf course as I could see a golf club in his hand and vast greens behind him. I turned my face away again.

"Hey sweetheart, just finished nine holes …so I …" and his voice got muted, as by then the lady had put on her ear plugs, and leaned back on the huge leather sofas. Now I could see the screen more clearly. I went back to flipping through the glossy magazine, but I could hear her talking with the punctuations of giggles.

"Of course, we are meeting, Naveen. I have taken off today …. just for you." The lady replied like a young girl in love, "I am heading a huge team, in a big firm, you know it. They say Natasha is a synonym for punctuality."

She heard him say something and then suddenly moved little ahead and said, "Oh, you can see? Yessss … I am in a salon."

The lady, that was Natasha, that I knew by then; looked around to check what else was visible to the caller. The screen was completely visible to me once again. The man that was Naveen, was indeed a handsome man and had a halo of being successful in his profession.

'What is he doing on the golf greens on a weekday? He is not that old…. may be some business deal.' My thoughts were churning in my mind. No wonder, my sons always quipped, "You are like Ms. Marple."

"Should I become a detective? Now, that I am retired?" I would ask my sons and my husband, who would pull my leg for my inquisitive nature and unnecessary curiosity in the happenings and people around us. Mostly I would end up predicting correctly about people.

"Madam, please come. It is ready." A young girl wearing a fresh apron and hair tied back in a bun, came and asked me to follow her to one of the cabins in the salon.

I felt rejuvenated after the facial. I walked towards another section of the salon for pedicure and manicure. There were huge reclining chairs in a row and I was surprised to see Natasha there. Her hair treatment had given her hair a different look. They were shinning and bouncy and had golden brown waves. She certainly knew what she wanted. We smiled at each other and took the chairs. As soon as we sat, another woman joined us, on the next chair.

'Women are so well dressed all the time.' I thought. This woman, who had just joined me and Natasha; was delicate and beautiful. She had fair, translucent skin, and had sharp features. She looked little older than Natasha. She was in an expensive pastel pink, embroidered pashmina kurta and trousers and looked very elegant. She had long shiny and smooth straight hair. She had only one ring on the finger of her left hand. It was a delicate ring with a solitaire as in contrast to Natasha, who wore big rings with big stones. This lady was petite and looked little tensed. She looked lost but she smiled looking at me. She then asked for an eye band and immediately rested on the reclined chair of hers.

I had only Natasha to speak with. I tried my luck, "I am the old one with grey hair between the two beauties."

"But you are so graceful! …. this is how I would like to be when I reach your age." Natasha replied very politely.

I felt very good. I looked at her and was about to say with a gesture of my hand, as if I was trivialising, 'Aah, you will be much smarter and better looking at my age.'

But then I again remembered my friend Payal who would often say, "Learn to say thanks and appreciate the compliments for the looks. You, dry Professor."

"Thank you" I said to Natasha, "But you look so amazing yourself. I am sure you will look the same even in my age." I did not know if I had played well.

Natasha smiled and thanked me. Our mutual appreciation banter was done and I was looking for another thread for the conversation. I never felt devoid of topics in any surroundings.

Lights were bright in this section of the salon as the beauticians needed to see our hands and feet well. Soft music was playing. I looked at my left. The lady looked so delicate and her skin so tender and fair that it seemed if somebody touched her, her skin would get dirty.

She suddenly removed her eye cover and looked at her feet. She then discussed what treatment she wanted with one of the beauticians. The shade of the nail paint she wanted. She seemed quite regular as she was indulging in mundane conversation with the employees in the salon. She was asking about their well-being. She knew many of them by name, that suggested that she was an old client

The manicure for all of us, was done; while our feet were soaked in water. Both the ladies on either side of me happily reached towards their phones. I asked for a magazine. Natasha put on some music on her phone, wore her ear pods, put on her eye mask and leaned back on the backrest.

The petite lady, whose name I did not know; asked the girl to fix her blue tooth in her ears and placed both her hands on the arm rest of the chair, fondly looking at her hands and nails. She seemed to have called her friend, "Yes, Aastha .... Naveen has gone to Mumbai for a few days. I have decided to give him a surprise. I am flying to Mumbai tomorrow morning."

Ms. Marple in me was curious. 'Naveen??!!' I wondered, how come these two ladies on either side of me, have a man in their life with the same name?

'Oh, dear .... Naveen is not in Mumbai. He is here in Delhi.' I almost told her but professor took over and said, 'Stop it .... stop your imagination!'

Ms. Marple in me held back and sat quietly.

The petite lady continued, "You are right Aastha .... I am sooo lucky to have him as my husband. Yes, he is on a business trip to meet some collaborators and they are finalising the deal in Golf link, Mumbai ... I will call you later." She disconnected the call and looked at her home screen with affection. And I could see her home screen. It showed the picture of the same Naveen with whom Natasha was speaking and was going to meet him in the evening.

The magazine slipped from my grip, and fell straight into the tub, in which my feet were soaked.

"Shut your mouth Professor, or a fly will go in," Ms. Marple chuckled.

Nuptial Bond

Shubham was very happy for his sister, Shweta, who was getting married. She was older to him by six years. His parents were looking for a suitable alliance for her for quite some time and were getting impatient in the process as she was already thirty-two. They were willing to accept if their children chose their life partner from a different region, religion, language, cast, culture or Nationality. Among the children of their friends' and relatives' many had chosen their life partners from foreign lands like Germany, China and America.

His mother often told his sister, "I thought, like all your friends, you too will choose your life partner on your own." She always secretly wished for that to happen.

Shweta had a couple of relationships but things had not worked out.

"Shubham, I have not met anyone, whom I would like to spend my whole life with." Shweta would often confide in his brother.

"Di, but your past relationships ... I found them good. In fact, the last one was very well placed." Shubham said.

"Yes, he was. But his parents were financially dependent on him. I know what happens in a longer run. Such boys feel so indebted to their parents that they focus more on them than their own families. I can't take that financial burden. In another case, the family was very rich but it was a huge joint family." Shweta shuddered at the thought and spoke in a matter-of-fact tone.

"I don't understand, how do you girls decide? Love doesn't matter?" Shubham was confused.

"Love? ha …" Shweta mocked. She then circled her hand pointing around, "Our parents' house, this bungalow, is going to be yours one day. Should I not make sure, that after marriage, I also continue to live my life with the same status that I am used to? I want a well earning man as my husband in my life." Shweta had said bluntly.

Shubham reacted, "Can't you earn and achieve the status yourself? What about compatibility? Or money will compensate everything?"

He paused for a moment and said, "Shweta di…. If you think, I will inherit our parents' house, this bungalow, … I will also have to take care of our parents in their old age. Then again," he looked at her and asked, "Now daughters too have equal right in their parents' property, what about that?" Shubham snickered.

"Shubham, don't be so condescending. You don't understand, how does it feel to leave everything behind and then suddenly make another household and family to be yours. There needs to be a great compensation for that." Shweta had said as a final statement.

"Ok." Shubham said. He wanted to speak further but he did not.

Shweta had been working after her graduation from a reputed engineering college. Shubham was still studying in the college. He started to cook, whenever he was alone at home, while both his parents and his siter were out for work. Within a couple of years Shubham had not just learned cooking but cooked delicious meals. He also acquired the skills of housekeeping.

When Shweta saw her brother cooking so well, and keeping the place clean, she pulled his leg, "Your wife would be lucky to have you …. but be careful, she will make you do everything and will not even enter the kitchen." Shweta said with a scornful laughter.

"What do you want? If men don't cook then you have a problem, if they cook then you have problem?" He had asked her back.

Eventually Shubham graduated and got the job. He worked for a couple of years, then took an education loan, when he got admission in a renowned school of business for studying MBA.

-::-

When Shweta liked everything about the alliance that was suggested to her, everybody at home were happy. Wedding preparations were on. Shweta wanted each event of her wedding to be special. According to the theme that she and her fiancé had finalised. Shubham was running around to book pre-wedding shoots, helping Shweta to finalise the choreographer, select an event management company. Their parents were busy making the lists of guests and gifts to be given. They were also managing the bill payments. Shubham was not in agreement the way his parents' hard-earned money was being spent so fast.

Sometimes Shubham would join Shweta and parents for shopping on the weekends for the clothes, jewellery and the gifts to be given. With every expense, he kept getting detached from the happenings. Often, they all would go to a restaurant for lunch or a tea break; when exhausted with the tedious process of looking, selecting and finalising the things to be bought.

During one such tea break, Shubham asked, "Papa, why are you spending so extravagantly on everything? This is your and Mom's life earnings, that you are going to be spending within a few days."

"Beta, we have been saving for this. See, a grand wedding of their daughter, is not just a duty but a dream of her parents." His father said.

Shubham could not believe his father. He had always known his parents as progressive. They always used to emphasise on a good higher education and encouraged them to acquire more academic qualifications while they could.

Shubham argued, "Instead of spending on wedding, you can keep that money for her future. It would be an investment wisely done." He then looked at his sister and asked, "Di, don't you find it a way too much?"

"Why are you jealous, your wedding will also be magnificent." Shweta teased him while going through the samples of her dress on her phone, that the designer had sent.

"At whose cost? And I am not jealous. Let this money be invested for you." Shubham said firmly.

"Everything is not about money; I want this dream wedding. And I have also saved some money from my earnings." Shweta now put the phone down and replied to her brother.

"Ha ..." Shubham knew that Shweta was not serious about her job and wanted to quit after her wedding. She wanted a comfortable life.

"I am not going to marry." He said, "And if I did, it would be a court marriage for sure. Such a wastage." He shook his head in disapproval.

"We will see." Shweta said in a sarcastic tone but had tears in her eyes.

Their father could not see his daughter being sad and he firmly told Shubham "No more comments about finances. Shubham, this is our decision as parents. Involve happily if you can or stay out of it."

Shubham understood, and he did not say anything even when the venue selected was little beyond their budget. Shweta and her fiancé were thrilled to see the place. He dutifully worked during his sister's wedding and made sure that the guests were looked after well. All the events went well. Wedding was a series of grand celebrations. The guests were praising the arrangements. Shubham did feel good as he realised that his parents had planned meticulously for the wedding to be a success. But he was not in the favour of unnecessary expenses and he did not want this for himself.

-::-

Since his days in high school, Shubham had started sensing the duality in the society. His restlessness made him write speeches and articles, both about political and social issues. He was disappointed to see that how independence had such a limited meaning for most of the girls who used to cheer him for his speeches. He wondered, that why he was not seeing girls he knew, using their independence to change the society?

"Do you only want to earn money and shop and travel and call it independence?" he had once quipped in his office café.

"Yes, why not?" his female colleague had argued.

"Earn money, enjoy the life… and don't get married. Marriage is a slavery." She took a sip of coffee and smiled at Shubham.

"Ok, fine …but then do something concrete. You are only living for yourself." Shubham said.

"What are you doing, Shubham? Staying with your parents in their house and giving us lectures." One female colleague remarked derisively.

Shubham could not say anything. He had realised, he needed to make a strong foothold before he could opine. That is when he had decided to study further to move ahead in his career. He studied and secured a management degree from a reputed school of business. After Shweta's wedding, he moved to Mumbai for his next job and exceled in his career very fast.

-::-

Shubham liked his life in Mumbai. He found that people were far more practical and had a no-nonsense approach in life. Nothing was on sly, whatever was there, was on the face. It had been a few years and Shubham was well settled in Mumbai. His social and work circles were expanding. In one of the business parties, he was introduced to Aditi. She worked in an audit firm and was very ambitious. She talked about the impact of certain policies of the government on the business and mostly was involved in shop talk. Still there was something in her that attracted Shubham and he could sense that the feeling was mutual. They enjoyed talking with each other and they decided to meet for lunch on Sunday. Each meeting led to another date. Once, their conversation steered towards personal and family life, when they were having lunch in their favourite Italian restaurant.

"You are smart, well educated, well placed and have a great personality. How come you are not married yet?" Aditi asked.

"May be, my definition of marriage does not have many suitors." Shubham chuckled. He poured some more wine in their glasses, "What about you? You are smart, attractive and well placed too." he asked her.

"I think the last one is the hurdle!" She laughed, picked up her glass and looked at him. "Actually, I was so busy making my career, that I never really thought about it. And now I am so used to my life all by myself, I can't even imagine bringing any changes to it. Plus, I have my parents' responsibility ...." she then looked at manicured lawns outside through huge glass window for a while.

"I don't know, why I said that! My parents always wanted me to be married. They are true Mumbaikars, so to say, practical and independent." She shrugged her shoulders, picked up pasta with her fork and said,

"Telling about parents kept the alliances at bay ..." she laughed heartily, "...and now they don't come anymore."

"So, does that make you feel bad?" Shubham asked.

"What? No!" She quickly replied.

"I am not a marriage material, how cliché it may sound, but I can't really see myself as a wife and as a mother, which is a natural progression for a woman in a marriage." Aditi took a bite of pasta.

Shubham looked at her and he felt something for her but kept it to himself. Both of them were in mid-thirties and had had their share of relationships. They both were quiet for a while eating their pasta.

He took a sip of his wine and said, "I want to be with someone, who could challenge me intellectually. With whom I could enjoy the conversation and life. Who is a separate person herself, not some little girl trapped in a grownup body."

"Oh!" Aditi chuckled, "And my fiercely independent personality traits were not much liked in my past relationships."

Shubham and Aditi went on holidays together. Once Aditi took him to introduce to her parents, who liked him a lot. A few days later, Shubham invited Aditi home for dinner. Aditi liked his well-kept apartment. She saw various artefacts picked up from different places in the country and abroad. She was impressed to see his book collection, neatly arranged in two tall book shelves kept on either side of the window.

"Bachelor pad to be messy is a stereo type, that we men promote like fools." Shubham said, when he saw Aditi looking around the house.

"I think, people liked that idea …. It is seen as a manly thing." Aditi said with a smirk "So convenient, isn't it?" Aditi sat on a sofa and asked him.

"So that a woman could take pride in bringing some order in his life. That became her job." Shubham went into the kitchen and opened the fridge.

"And in return, he took care of her like a child." She got up and sat on a high chair kept near the platform, dividing dining area and the kitchen. They both smiled at each other and enjoyed the way conversation was flowing.

"Mutual dependency?" He took out a bottle from the fridge and placed it on the table.

"Do you think it worked for the previous generations?" She looked at the bottle then asked him.

"I don't know. I don't think there is any fixed formula for things to work." He said removing two goblets from the shelf of the small bar, kept near the table.

"Hmm … true that. Each one of us is so different." Aditi looked around and saw a couple of photo frames in Shubham's book shelf.

"My parents and my sister and her family." Shubham said.

"Shubham, your house is so well kept, wow!" Aditi praised.

"Thank you, Ma'am, hope you like the food as well." He said and went to the kitchen

Pasta was ready. He brought hot pasta on the table and poured white wine for both. They sat and had their dinner with heartfelt conversation. Later Shubham put on some music and showed her some books. They found themselves standing too close to each other but none of them moved away. Shubham held her face and Aditi closed her eyes. Shubham gently kissed her and Aditi kissed him back. They kissed passionately and embraced each other for long.

'It is so liberating to be with someone who is a complete self, I think we should be good together.' Same thought echoed in their mind.

-::-

Parents of both, Aditi and Shubham were happy to see their children getting married. It was a court marriage and a small party was thrown, where only their friends, few colleagues and first relations were present. Their life resumed after their honeymoon in a very natural way. Neither Shubham nor Aditi tried to change each other. They both collectively invested in a new apartment that was equally close to their respective work place.

Shubham and Aditi, both had the same thought about extending their family. Neither of them wanted to have children. Aditi had to travel a lot for her projects. Shubham was promoted and became the country head for his company. Their parents had stopped asking about baby as they had realised that both Shubham and Aditi were different from usual couples and were very strong headed.

After a couple of years Shubham and Aditi decided to host a Diwali gathering and invite both sides of the family. They realised they were totally taken up by their demanding careers and needed to take a break to spend time with their families. Their parents were overjoyed to join them and so was Shweta.

-::-

Aditi, who would mostly be in the office wear or in simple track pants and a t-shirt at home, was beaming in a traditional attire. Shubham also wore traditional kurta and pyjama.

"Today you both are looking like one of us." Shubham's father joked in the evening, when they all were was sitting in the living room, after lighting the lamps. Everybody laughed. They all had their meal together, were awake till late talking, playing board games with Shweta's children.

It was almost two at night, when everybody went to sleep. Aditi and Shubham were in their room, happy and content.

"It feels good, isn't it? To have our family around and celebrate together." Aditi said and went near Shubham, turning her back to him. She pulled her hair in front and asked Shubham to open the knot of her top at the back. Shubham pulled the red and gold strings and gently kissed her bare back.

"Yes ... it feels good." He whispered in her ears.

Aditi giggled as she felt tickled. "Arre, I meant …" she turned around and looked at him and said, "You are looking like a prince in this Kurta."

"And you, a queen." Shubham pulled Aditi towards him and planted a kiss.

"Should I not be a princess, if you are a prince?" Aditi caressed his face and asked with a twinkle in her eyes. Shubham held her in his arms and they both kissed passionately, made love, snuggled up and slept happily.

After Diwali, their parents and Shubham's sister and her family left and their usual routine resumed. A few weeks passed.

-::-

Aditi was tensed. She once again looked at her report. She paced restlessly across their room. Shubham was trying to calm her down.

"No, no, Shubham!" She showed him the file. "How did it happen? ….. No, it is so scary …. I... I can't. I am not ready for this. I can never be ready for this. We can't be pregnant. I don't want this."

She panicked.

"Listen, do not tell either side of the parents …. I... I … they will force me to keep the baby ……" Aditi held her head and sat on the sofa.

Shubham was still trying to grasp the situation. He too did not want to plan a family but now he was not sure of his feelings. He thought, 'Even if now, I want, it is Aditi, who has to go through all of this, she has to bear the pain and the consequences.'

He sat near Aditi and held her at shoulders, "Don't worry, if you don't want …. we won't have. We will go to the hospital and get done with it."

Aditi moved her head up and looked at him in a disbelief. She asked angrily, "What do you mean by if I don't want? …. You mean, you want it now? …. So, now I also have to go through the guilt of aborting the pregnancy all by myself? …...Wow! Shubham, when did you change?" Her eyes welled up and she felt cheated.

Shubham was shocked and silent. He felt Aditi was right.

"We both started walking together because our thoughts about major things in life were same …. and…. and now you suddenly became like 'You and I'?" Aditi was upset.

Shubham's head was spinning. He found himself at the crossroads.

'I know, I am wrong …. but I need some time to get over it.' He thought.

Aditi was suddenly feeling alone. That night they did not speak with each other. It was for the first time that they had such stressful night.

-::-

Aditi booked an appointment in a renowned hospital and informed Shubham in the office. They both reached there on time.

He was waiting in the Doctor's cabin, when Aditi came out of the check-up room. Doctor waited for her to sit next to Shubham and then explained them the situation. Because of Aditi's age and certain medical conditions, abortion was risky. She advised them to go ahead with the pregnancy as Aditi had already passed the major portion of her fertile years. Maybe in future when they would want, it might not be possible for her to conceive. She asked them to think over it.

Both Aditi and Shubham decided to take a second opinion. Aditi also asked her friend who was a gynaecologist in the USA and sent her the reports. In their indecisiveness, few more days had passed.

Shubham had cleared his mind by then. He went to Aditi's office, and they both went to a restaurant. He chose a quiet corner, ordered fresh fruit juice for both of them and sat next to Aditi.

"Aditi, I am with you. I want whatever you want. I can't think of anything at the cost of you. I don't want to lose you. Now you have to decide, what you want. We are together." He held her hands and spoke softly and firmly.

Aditi had calmed down by then.

"You may find it strange, Shubham… I have decided to go ahead with the pregnancy but I can't be a traditional mother. In fact, there was a time that I did not even want to be a wife, but here I am." She looked at him.

"Will you be there for our child?" She asked him.

"Of course." Shubham said. "That goes unsaid, why are you asking this?"

"I will need separation.... let's separate." Aditi suddenly said.

Shubham was not prepared for this. He looked at her with shock.

Aditi was in tears. She said with a lump in her throat, "Shubham, I love you…....but all this is too much for me. I want to lead a free life. …. I ... I don't know how to tell you." She started sobbing.

Shubham held her hands tight. They both had tears in their eyes.

'It is all hormonal, maybe…' Shubham secretly wished.

They both came home and slept holding each other quietly. Their routine resumed like before, more calmly now when the decision was made. Shubham often thought of her sister, whom he used to ridicule for wanting to quit the job and get into full time home and family management.

"You only want comfort at the cost of others." He used to tease her. He had a rueful smile at the irony of his life.

Shubham was constantly thinking about the future life that he had to face post Aditi's delivery. He was already well established and there was no problem on financial front. He thought of working from home.

Aditi delivered a healthy baby boy and everybody in the family were happy. Aditi had resumed her office and Shubham was surprised that she had not developed any special bond with their son. She had taken up new projects and had moved on with her growth in the career.

Shubham had taken a sabbatical from his job and eventually shifted to consultancy job that allowed him to work from home at flexible hours. He had hired a nanny, but he made sure, always to be at home.

Shubham cooked, played with his son. He took the charge of his vaccination, food chart, visits to paediatrician. His book shelves now had baby books.

One evening Aditi returned home and asked Shubham if their son was sleeping. Shubham asked her to go and see herself but she refused. She asked Shubham to sit as she wanted to talk with him.

She took out a file from her bag and handed it over to him.

He opened the file, read the divorce papers, signed and gave the file back to her. They both looked at each other and held their emotions.

Aditi took the papers and walked out.

Shubham went into his room and saw his son was awake in his cradle. He picked him up, and kissed him gently. His son chuckled and held Shubham's finger with his tiny fist. Shubham lovingly looked at him and gently kissed on his head and softly whispered,

"Now on, it is our journey, you and me, we will make it great together."

Heirloom

Sunanda had come to stay with her youngest daughter, Sakshi; for a few days. Sakshi's daughter, Anaya was getting married in a month's time. Sunanda's husband, who had retired as a senior surgeon, was supposed to come a week before the wedding. He had decided to work, even after his retirement, as a senior consulting doctor to a renowned hospital of the city. Both Sunanda and her husband were in their seventies and lived independently.

Sunanda had her siesta and woke up feeling fresh. She washed her face, combed her hair, pulled it back and tied neatly in a bun. She sprinkled some talcum powder around her neck and put a bindi on her forehead. She changed into a saree, draped it well. Sunanda felt cold, so she wore her woollen socks and slip-ons. She picked up the tube kept on her bedside table and applied cream on her arms and hands. Sunanda wrapped her shawl that was kept neatly folded near her pillow. She walked through the huge living room and the dining room then entered the kitchen of her daughter's big house. Her daughter Sakshi was there, busy with some work.

Sunanda sat on the chair, kept near the table placed in the centre of the kitchen. She rubbed her palms and said,

"I like the smell of this cream, that you had kept by my bedside. This keeps my hands so soft. What do you call it? ... hand cream, right? I like it."

She then asked mischievously, "Do they have this for every part of the body, Sakshi? Like knee cream, elbow cream, chin cream or for feet?"

Sunanda made an innocent face and then stared at her daughter, Sakshi, who was busy arranging the grocery items which were just delivered. Sakshi smiled discreetly; she knew her mother was trying to make her laugh. Her mother never liked the serious atmosphere and sombre faces. She always tried to lighten up the mood of everyone with her humour.

Seeing no reaction from Sakshi, Sunanda laughed on her own questions. She rested her elbows on the table and keenly watched Sakshi, who was removing grocery items from the cotton bags kept on the marble top of the table.

"I like your kitchen. So big, so spacious, so airy with big windows." Sunanda again tried to connect with her daughter.

"Yes. Ma, that was one thing, I always wanted," Sakshi finally responded to her mother while directing her domestic help to stack the things in the pantry.

"Hmm and when you open any kitchen cabinet, the light inside gets on! One can easily see and eat whatever snack one wants to eat, but nothing home-made!" Sunanda quipped and looked at her daughter with the corner of her eye.

"Maa? Who has the time? And besides, I am done now. I am fifty!" Sakshi was slightly irritated. She was far from her mother's cooking skills.

Sunanda was an excellent cook. She was known for her culinary skills. Her homemade sweets and savouries were liked by everyone in the family. She enjoyed looking after her home, raising her children, trying out different recipes, meeting new people and dressing up nicely. She did not like that her daughter, Sakshi bought readymade snacks.

"Oh yes, you poor old lady .... No, wait, what do they call now?" Sunanda questioned and took her arms inside her shawl.

"Middle age crisis!" Sakshi said and looked at her help, Nilu, who was a few years younger than her.

Nilu looked at Sunanda and said, "I am also going through that, Maa ji, what just didi said. I can't work as fast as I could do earlier. But Maa ji you look so fresh and ...."

"Keep quiet and focus on your work, Nilu! Do you even know the meaning of mid age cri ... forget it." Sakshi scolded her help.

"No, no, let her finish. I look fresh and, what?" Sunanda asked Nilu with a naughty smile and a curiosity. Nilu looked at Sakshi and hesitated to answer. But Sunanda insisted, "Tell me ..."

"And hot ...." Nilu answered sheepishly and giggled.

"Hot?... I am feeling cold." Sunanda laughed.

"Don't act smart Nilu. Nothing Ma, she wants a compliment for herself. She thinks she still looks like an eighteen-year-old when she is forty-two." Sakshi feigned anger and looked at Nilu with a smile.

"What? You are forty-two? I thought, you must be fifty-two!!" Sunanda said dramatically and burst into a laughter again.

Sakshi could not control her laughter either, looking at Nilu's face.

Seeing them both laugh, confused Nilu joined their laughter.

It had started drizzling. Sakshi sent Nilu to get the clothes from the terrace and iron them. Nilu immediately left the kitchen.

"I will make some tea, Ma," Sakshi said.

"Yes, it is getting cold. And it is tea time anyway." Sunanda said and rubbed both her palms, then looked at the back of her hands again. She looked at the veins seen through her pale delicate wrinkled skin.

"Don't these veins tell you the journey of my life!" She smiled and looked at Sakshi.

Sakshi did not respond. She found her mother's self-love little irritating at times but she knew, that, this attitude of her mother had kept her mentally and physically fit even at this age.

"Yes, yes ... I know, you don't like me telling all this over and again." Sunanda could sense her daughter's irritation.

"No Maa…" Sakshi regretted for not responding to her, but she was quite exhausted with the preparations for her daughter's wedding. Though she felt that her mother, Sunanda had turned the atmosphere relaxed with her light hearted conversations.

"This was delivered while you were sleeping." She patted the bags and looked at her mother, who looked so elegant and lively at her age. Sakshi pondered if she would ever reach her mother's age. 'Would I look this elegant and be half as fit as she is, at her age?' she thought looking at her mother.

"Ma, you look fresh! It seems you had a sound sleep." Sakshi poured water in the vessel for making tea.

"Hmmm, I indeed had a nice nap," said Sunanda then caressed the top of the table, "This table is beautiful, with drawers and shelves underneath. Nice marble top. You have some name for this table, isn't it?" Sunanda asked Sakshi.

Sakshi looked at Sunanda and was lost for the word. "This table? yes ... oh, I am just blank." She said and started pounding the ginger hastily, with little exasperation and a chuckle that was ironic and ticklish both.

-::-

Sakshi's daughter, Anaya entered the kitchen. She hugged Sunanda lovingly, "Naani …. It feels so good to have you around." She then looked at her mother who was pounding ginger while water kept on the gas stove was boiling.

"Mom, water must have reduced by a cup now, look at the ginger … it has turned into a fine paste!" She giggled.

"Stop making fun of me. You make tea now," she said and pushed the pestle and mortar towards Anaya. Mortar slid smoothly on the black granite top of the kitchen.

"I am fogged again." Sakshi was puzzled. She pulled the stool and sat next to her mother, Sunanda.

Anaya added two more cups of water to the pot and said with a big smile and a spark in her eyes, "I will add some cardamom too."

"Add whatever you want to add, but make tea, that is all I want now." said Sakshi and started removing the grocery items from the cotton bags.

Anaya arranged the tea cups in one tray and poured tea in the kettle. She then took out ginger cookies from the cabinet and placed them in a plate. When she placed the tray with tea kettle, cups and cookies on the table, a whiff of ginger spread in the air and the three ladies sitting around it smiled looking at each other.

Sakshi was still trying to remember the word for the table while she poured the tea from the kettle. She took a sip of tea and closed her eyes.

"Aaah ...tea is heavenly!" then she smiled at her daughter.

"You don't need any makeup; you are glowing in love." Sunanda said and then nudged her granddaughter, "So, what is his name?", she asked mischievously.

"Naani!!" Anaya exclaimed and answered, "His name is Anish. You know it." She smiled.

Anaya took a sip of tea and asked Sunanda, "Naani, did you ever fall in love?"

Before Sunanda could reply, Sakshi looked at Anaya's happy face and told her mother, "You know, Ma … I am so happy and satisfied. Everything has fallen into right place. Anaya has found not only a good life partner in Anish, but also a very loving, cultured, well-educated and progressive family. Anaya's father is also very happy with the alliance, as Anaya will continue working in her field."

"Yes, Nani, because Anish's grandpa has already offered me a position in their business. He, in fact everybody in their family believes that education and skills should be put to best use." Anaya said happily.

"No wonder, with such great thoughts, the business that Anish's grandpa had started; next generations took it ahead." Sakshi was overwhelmed.

Anaya saw her mother's eyes had welled up. She held her mother's hand and turned towards her grand ma and asked again,

"Arre, Naani …. you tell me, did you ever have a fling?"

"Means?" Sunanda looked puzzled and asked.

"Naani, mom tells me that someone had proposed you but you were already engaged to Grandpa. What is the story, Naani? Grandpa is not here; you can tell." Anaya asked mischievously.

"Your grandpa knows all about it. ... and at this age no one bothers. We even begin to forget what we had spoken a day before....." Sunanda laughed and looked like she was lost in some thoughts. Anaya patted her hand and coaxed her to tell the story.

"Your Grandpa is my first love. We had seen each other in a wedding. In fact, our parents had already decided to get us married and we did not know. Your grandpa was a doctor already and I was impressed." Sunanda said and moved her tea cup aside, as the tea was over.

"Naani, I want to know your proposal story that happened in your college!" Anaya poured some tea in Sunanda's cup and gave it to her.

"Oh that! .... I did not even know back then that it was a proposal." She trivialised the topic with her hand gesture.

"Come on, you could not be that innocent." Anaya laughed.

Sunanda took a sip and said, "I was in the University, studying in the final year of my post-graduation. There was a tall and fair young man, who looked like Shashi Kapoor ..."

"Who is Shashi Kapoor?" Anaya interrupted.

"He was a Bollywood star of those times." Sakshi said. She often felt sidelined, whenever her mother and her daughter got talking. So, she had resumed her work in the kitchen.

"Oh ... okay." Anaya said to her mother and looked at her grandmother.

Sunanda took a sip from her tea cup and looked at Anaya with love.

-::-

That was the year around mid-sixties. Sunanda was studying for masters. After the final exams, students had gathered for a group photograph in one of the lawns in the campus of the university. Sunanda saw a tall, fair and handsome young man with green eyes, standing there. Later, when Sunanda was sitting in the lawn along with her friends, that young man approached Sunanda.

He hesitantly handed over a small packet to Sunanda and said, "This is for you, please keep it." Sunanda involuntarily took it.

Then he immediately turned and walked away. Sunanda opened the packet in front of her friends. It had a diary and a small wooden box with intricate carving. Her friends asked her to open the diary and the box, but she packed it again.

She got up. "Why did I accept it? I will return this to him. Why did he give this to me and walked away?" Sunanda wondered.

"He is from another department. Maybe, he likes you." Her friend teased her.

She took one of her friends along and looked for him but they could not find him.

Sunanda brought the packet home and kept in her room. At night, in her room she quietly opened the small box and she was astonished to see a beautiful ring of gold with an oval shaped ruby studded in it. She then opened the diary. There was a letter inside. She opened the letter; it was addressed to her in a beautiful hand writing.

"Sunanda, I am directly writing to you. You are a nice person. I admire you. I want to spend my life with you. I am nothing at present but I have plans to make a good future and I believe, I will. The box contains my mother's ring. She is no more but she had given this to me to give it to the love of my life. Will you walk this life with me?"

In the next para, he had shared all the details about him, his family and had written that he would inform his father and her parents, if she agrees. At the end of the page, he had written his name, Rajdeep Sehgal.

Sunanda's heart beats increased. She smiled and felt strange but liked the admiration from a young man. She showed it to her mother. Her mother asked her to return the letter and the ring both to the young man from her college, so that he would understand her intentions.

Sunanda's house was buzzing with the preparations for her wedding. Just a week before her wedding day, there was convocation ceremony in her university. Sunanda and her friends had worn their beautiful sarees. Sunanda had done her hair in a bouffant, had worn gold earrings and carried a conical purse gifted to her by her aunt. She wore kajal and tucked a flower in her bun.

After the ceremony, Sunanda met Rajdeep. He was looking smart and dashing in a white shirt and brown trousers with a narrow leather belt. He was wearing a dark brown coat. His hair was well done. When Sunanda saw him, she kept looking at him.

Sunanda opened her purse, took out the packet and gave that to Rajdeep.

"Did you read?" he asked. He looked mesmerised by her beauty.

Before Sunanda could reply, her friend came and pulled her by elbow, "Sunanda, Lets go to the studio.... We will have a photograph taken with our degree and in this gown!"

"Yes, let us go." Sunanda replied with a trailing gaze at Rajdeep, when her friend dragged her through the corridor of the college.

Rajdeep kept looking at them walking away from him. He was looking hurt.

-::-

Sunanda took a sip of tea and looked at her granddaughter.

"Wow, Naani ...your mom was so cool! Back then, she did not scold you upon seeing a love letter, written to you!!" Anaya said and hugged her grandmother. She then looked at her own mother.

"Yes, you team up against me." Sakshi understood her daughter's expressions.

"What a beautiful story, Naani! …. but you certainly broke his heart. That is bad." Anaya told her grandmother.

"Anaya! Naani had no feelings for him." Sakshi clarified.

"Only if she had given some time to herself! Also, why did that man wait so long until her graduation? Mom .... at least she could have replied to him. He probably never knew if Naani read that letter." Anaya said.

"I got married to your grandfather immediately after my post-graduation. So, he might have known that I was not meant for him." Sunanda said.

"How cruel. He took so much pain. You should have at least told him that you had read the letter .... his feelings would have got some closure." Anaya said tapping on the table. She was restless.

"Now! this is the problem with your generation, you get too much in psychology." Sakshi said, and picked up the tray.

Sunanda was quiet. She looked at her granddaughter then turned towards her daughter and said something that surprised both Sakshi and Anaya,

"I think, she is right, Sakshi. He deserved an answer."

Sunanda stared out of the window for a while quietly then she got up slowly, "I am feeling exhausted. I will rest for a while now. Don't disturb me."

Sakshi told her daughter, "Now your Naani would like to be all by herself on her own island. .... Island? .... Yesss, Island it is!!"

Sakshi suddenly felt happy, smacked the table top and called out her mother, "Maaa... this table is called, Kitchen Island! You had asked, this table has a name ...."

Sunanda was out of the kitchen already, walking slowly and steadily. But she heard Sakshi. She raised her hand and waved gently.

Anaya raised her brows and was completely clueless about what her mother had just said and how the emotion of love had just faded away from the conversation.

-:::-

Sakshi had invited the whole family of Anaya's would be in-laws for an informal dinner. She thought, it would be nice if all the generations of both the families met each other in an informal environment.

After dinner, everybody was sitting in the drawing room discussing the events and the ceremonies of the wedding. Sakshi asked her help to make coffee for all.

"Anaya, come here," called her mother-in-law to be, with love.

Anaya got up and sat next to her.

"This is given to the daughters-in-law of our family. To the love of sons in our family. An old tradition." Her mother-in-law smiled and took out a small wooden box with intricate carving on it, from her handbag. She placed it on Anaya's palm and asked her to open it.

Anaya opened the box. There was a beautiful gold ring with an oval shaped Ruby studded in it. Anaya was astonished to see the box and the ring in it.

Anaya looked at her Naani, Sunanda, who was looking beautiful and elegant in her pastel pink saree and a pearl string around her neck. She was sipping her coffee and was talking to Anaya's grandfather-in-law.

He was indeed a fair, tall and a handsome old man with green eyes.

'Oh my god! Anish's grandfather? Rajdeep!' Anaya was overwhelmed and looked at them. They both raised their coffee cups and smiled at her.

Anaya smiled back as her fiancé Anish put the ring on her finger.

"To the love of my life." He whispered in her ears.

Reunion

Pranjal held her hair up in her fist, gave a twist to it and fixed one clutch to hold them up tightly. Then she wore her spectacles and bent forward to observe herself minutely in the mirror. She looked at her skin, turned her face to left and to right. She smiled as she saw her fresh glowing face.

She spoke with her image in the mirror, "Not bad, Pranjal! This is the best you can look in your fifties!" She then looked into the mirror and caressed the mole on her left shoulder; she remembered how her husband was amused when he had noticed it for the first time.

"It is only for me to see." He would kiss her gently, on her shoulder and would look at her with a fondness for her in his eyes. She would melt in his arms, looking into his eyes.

Pranjal shook her head and quickly moved towards her cupboard. She had already decided what to wear. It was a pleasant weather of February. The reunion was at noon. So, she had opted for pastel pink kurta and beige trousers in cotton silk.

'These are so, so comfortable, with pockets on both the sides. Ah! so good!' She thought every time, she wore comfort fitting trousers. Pranjal had never sought big things in her life. She would celebrate little things in her day-to-day life.

-::-

"You become happy even in small things, one should learn this from you. I really like that." Nitin had once said.

He was very impressed with her efforts and resource management in setting up their one room apartment. Pranjal had decked up the place within two days. It was a makeshift living arrangement in the Army base camp, where his unit was constructing a strategic road and a bridge in the hilly region.

"Sweetheart, you deserve the best." Nitin had bent over to kiss her before leaving for his duty.

"I have the best, Captain Nitin." Pranjal had said with a pride on her face and a twinkle in her eyes. She gently caressed the name tab on her husband's uniform before seeing him off.

Time flew by. Pranjal had to live alone whenever Nitin had a field posting. She had to play the roles of both father and mother for their children. She took pride in what Nitin always said, "Never label your duty as sacrifice." She saw Nitin working day and night with a smile on his face. This had percolated to their children too.

Both their children studied well and had flown away to make their own nests. Nitin and Pranjal had decided to settle in Delhi after his retirement. Due to social media, Pranjal had got in touch with many of her college friends. A reunion in the capital was planned by one of them. She was getting ready for that.

-::-

Pranjal was ready. She came out and sat in the living room. She checked her watch and thought, 'I get ready pretty fast now.' She looked out in the balcony. Nitin was reading a book. His steaming cup of tea was next to him. He seemed to have poured it himself from the electric kettle. Pranjal had setup a small tea station in her balcony with a cozy reading corner. A small book cabinet, on the top of which, she had kept a wooden box with varieties of tea bags in it, two mugs and a kettle always filled with water. One could make tea while sitting on the chair, reading a book. At night, the balcony would look cozier with a cane lamp hanging from the ceiling and a swing on the other end of the balcony with planters laid out. Pranjal smiled seeing Nitin immersed in the book.

Nitin turned and asked, "All set to go?"

"Yes, I should be back by five, max by six as many have to catch the night flight back home." Pranjal replied.

"Your friends seem quite bonhomie coming from different cities for this reunion." Nitin asked, closing the book with his finger still on the page he was reading.

"Not all. Actually, few of them are flying back to USA and meeting us on their stop-over. And some of them had come here for their work. One is here to attend a wedding, and remaining are from Delhi, Noida and Gurgaon." Pranjal paused for a moment and said, "Nitin, actually, I am not sure, if I should go."

"Why? Because of your arguments on your college social media group?" Nitin smiled.

"Yes." She said.

"But you did not say anything wrong, rather requested people not to spread hatred." He assured her.

"Hmm, you are right. I am happy that Zainab is coming. In that group, few of us grew up playing together. Still, some friends shared the messages that were communal in nature." Pranjal stared at her mobile and said, "I don't know where the world is heading now."

"You must go, Pranjal. Have a good time. And tell Dheeraj to serve me lunch by two." Nitin quickly normalised the atmosphere. Dheeraj, their house-help and an excellent cook, was with them for many years.

"I have told him." Pranjal smiled and went to the balcony, bent over and kissed her husband on his forehead. She picked up her hand bag and her car key, waved to Nitin and stepped out of her flat.

Pranjal reached on time as usual. She handed over the keys to the valet and entered the foyer of the hotel. She was happy to see that few of her college friends were already there, sitting in the lounge area. They almost screamed every time a classmate entered the foyer. They all greeted and hugged each other and immersed into conversation.

"We must thank Manish, who arranged everything," someone said.

"Where is he?" The other one asked.

"I had just seen him. Running around to check on the arrangements." Somebody answered.

After the initial euphoria, there was a little awkwardness too. For a moment Pranjal thought if she did right by agreeing to be part of the reunion. It was not an alumni reunion. She saw, the crowd at the foyer was eventually divided into small groups, mostly classmates, section wise or those who were in touch with each other. Some were trying to establish a connect. Pranjal could feel how the jobs, cities and countries had brushed the colour on each one of them. She sat on one of the sofas kept in the foyer.

Manish came and announced, "Ante room is ready. Let everyone come, then we will move to the hall."

"Sure, we will catch up here till then," said Nidhi, and sat on the sofa kept across Pranjal.

"Nidhi, you are running a fashion house, right?" Pranjal asked.

"You mean, a boutique." A friend quipped, before Nidhi could answer Pranjal.

"No, darling. It is on much higher scale. You must visit me in Bombay, here have my card." Nidhi explained the friend, who had given boutique remark, with a smile.

"Are visiting cards still in?" Somebody murmured.

"If you have one." Nidhi laughed, then turned to Pranjal, "Yes, I own a fashion house." And they both got talking.

Everybody's head turned, when they saw Ragini, who was married in a big business family, entering the foyer. Her diamonds were shinning, not just in her jewellery but on her handbag and watch too. Then came Vinita, dressed in an elegant cotton-silk saree. While Vinita was still walking towards her college friends, sitting on the couch, someone asked with a curiosity,

"She is Vinita, no? I think, she works in an NGO."

"She owns and runs one." Pranjal answered. She enjoyed the guessing and speculating game that started as soon as anyone from their group entered the foyer of the hotel.

Then came Zainab, elegantly dressed up in a business suit. There was a sudden silence in the group, upon seeing her. Zainab looked at everyone and waved with a big smile. She walked towards them, and was very happy when she saw Pranjal. She spread her arms and said,

"Hey Pranjal, how are you? So long!"

"Yes, so long!" Pranjal smiled and they both hugged each other. Zainab asked how was everybody doing. Pranjal was happy to see the warmth that Zainab brought and was relieved to feel an ease in the atmosphere. Manish came and announced with an excitement, "Let's move to the hall".

Everybody got up and Manish led them towards the hall. As they were crossing the huge foyer, she heard somebody whisper,

"These people are not trustworthy."

"Who do you mean by, these people?" Pranjal asked in a simple tone trying to keep a smile on her face.

"There she goes, the only patriotic person in our group." Someone said on a lighter note and there was a wave of laughter that travelled in a section of the group.

"Pranjal, we might not be in the Army but we are also patriotic." said Pankaj, who used to share messages of communal divide on the social media group. He supported the idea of religious identity for India, while both his children were settled in the USA and he was hoping them to become the citizens of America and relinquish Indian citizenship.

Pranjal thought of saying something but she had realised, it was of no use. She reminded herself that she was there just to have a good time as she had promised Nitin. She always objected whenever her friends from college, shared communal messages with the undercurrents of hatred. She firmly asked them not to do so. She would be disappointed in finding herself mostly alone in her efforts. Soon she realised that individual opinions did not matter if not in sync with a particular ideology.

"Pankaj, we NRIs are patriotic too and we love our country." Came a voice from behind.

"I know." Pankaj turned back and said, "Both my sons are also in San Francisco and they love India and Indian culture."

'How and why? By following the cultural and religious rituals?' Pranjal thought controlling her urge to speak. She kept walking with a smile.

Zainab looked at Pranjal and made things lighter with a laughter and said, "You know it, Pranjal, by 'these people', she means Muslims. Some think we are not Indians."

"Are we going to be next?" A male voice with a heavy baritone came from behind, followed by a laughter.

"Andrew!!??" Few ladies exclaimed and turned back to see. That was him. Tall and dusky Andrew D'Souza.

"Here comes our Remo Fernandes!" Few exclaimed. Andrew resembled a popular singer from Goa, during their college days. Pranjal saw Ragini's face had beamed.

"You had a crush on him, isn't it?" somebody nudged Ragini.

"Hello ladies! How are you? So nice to see all!" Andrew asked with an excitement.

"Hey, Andy!! Atta Cowboy !!" Manish, who was leading the group towards the party hall, turned back, walked past all the men and women in the group, and embraced him. Andrew lifted Manish and whirled. They were near a water fountain. Manish screamed,

"Put me down. We are not young …. we both will break our backs." Manish laughed but was concerned.

"Good show, yaar. Nice place." Andrew patted his back and looked around the open court yard of the hotel with café and fountains.

"I just managed; I am glad you all could make it. As for the place; well, Ali is the person to thank for. He is the owner of this hotel." Manish said, adjusting his clothes.

"Really?" Many in the group were surprised.

They all entered the party hall and sat around the tables. Everyone in the group reintroduced themselves, talking about the work they did, how far one had reached. How big they had made it. One woman felt apologetic, while other two proudly told that they were housewives. Pranjal was one of them. Eventually sub-groups were formed.

Nidhi, who had come from Bombay had no interest in political or social issues. She was only interested in the ideas of business expansion and making contacts. She was looking most glamourous among all. She had a soft corner for Pranjal. She picked up her wine and sat next to her and said,

"I have my flight tonight. If I had one more day, I would have explored Delhi with you."

"You must be visiting here a lot; we can do that." Pranjal said, though she knew, these were mere talks.

"Oh yes, I do come here quite often, for work, you know. Hey, how have you come? CO Saab has sent the gaadi?" Nidhi asked.

Pranjal could make out, Nidhi had no idea, where she was in her life. It had been quite some time since her husband had retired and one is CO at much younger age.

"No, I have driven here myself." Pranjal replied with a smile.

"That is so nice! …. you are pretty independent for a housewife!" Nidhi spoke in a patronising tone and got up excusing herself, "Hey, I will quickly catch up with the guys too." And she walked towards the group of men.

Pranjal had stopped responding to housewife remarks. Vinita was watching this. She moved near her.

"Why few women who make big money look down upon us, the housewives." She almost whispered in Pranjal's ears.

Pranjal looked at her and smiled. Just then Manish announced some game, that was followed by lunch. A few songs were sung by some of them. Everyone participated and enjoyed. Later tea and coffee were served. Pranjal picked up her cup and looked at her watch. It was almost four thirty. She met everyone, conveyed thanks to Manish for initiating a reunion and appreciated Ali for such fantastic arrangements in his grand hotel.

Manish offered to walk her out. She thanked him and said,

"Come on, you are not a host. Nobody is. You go back and enjoy. I will walk myself out. I am in my city."

Manish laughed and joined back the group.

Pranjal was missing Nitin. She gave the card to the valet, who brought her car in the porch. She was happy to drive back home.

Pranjal opened the door with her key. Nitin was in the living room, strumming his guitar. Country music was playing on the speakers. He was happy to see her back.

"What a timing!" He exclaimed, keeping his guitar aside. Just now I told Dheeraj, "Madam is about to come, make some tea."

"Oh dear!" Pranjal felt relieved. She removed her footwear, placed the keys in the bowl kept on the console table near the entrance. She walked in the living room, sat on the sofa next to Nitin.

"So, how was the reunion party?" Nitin asked.

"Made me long for this." She hugged Nitin.

"You must keep going out, I like this longing." Nitin winked at her.

Pranjal laughed, just then Dheeraj entered with a tray well set. His years of training had made him expert to place different snacks every time, with a tea pot and cups. Pranjal felt relaxed seeing the steam coming out of the spout of the kettle. Both of them drank their tea and she narrated the happenings at the reunion.

"I will quickly change then we will go for our evening walk." She said and felt a twinge.

Pranjal washed her face, changed in to her cotton trousers and cotton top. Kept her mobile in one pocket and house key in another. She wore her walking shoes and went to the living room. She saw, Nitin was ready with his shoes and jacket on.

"Ready, Colonel?" Pranjal asked.

"Yes, Madam." said Nitin with a smile.

Pranjal walked towards him and saw their reflection in the glass cover of the shelf, where Nitin's Shaurya chakra was placed along with the citation from the President of India. She kept her hand on Nitin's shoulder. He placed his palm on her hand and said nothing.

She then held the handles of his wheel chair and pushed gently to the main door.

"Dheeraj, don't forget to roast some makhana after making dinner and shut the door."

Whirlpool

Shubhangi and Milind were sitting on the chairs, in the backyard of a village homestay in the coastal region of Konkan, waiting for their morning tea. It was around seven in the morning.

They had reached the homestay the previous night. They were served fresh traditional Marathi food for dinner. Soon after, they had retired to bed as they were exhausted after a long road journey through the hilly region.

Shubhangi had woken up fresh in the morning and walked around their homestay. There were houses in a row, constructed in traditional and local architectural style. Each house had a tiled front-yard, bordered with flower beds. After crossing the front yard, one had to climb a few steps to enter the covered veranda. Shubhangi felt very comfortable in the simplicity of the place. Their homestay was a neat and clean house that had three bedrooms, with minimalistic décor.

A passage from common area led to the balcony at the back of the house. If one stood in the balcony, could see the backyard with a lot of coconut trees, stretching up to the sea shore. There were a few steps from the balcony to climb down to reach the backyard. The lady, who was the owner of the homestay, lived in the adjacent house.

Shubhangi was admiring the natural beauty, when her husband, Milind came in the backyard and sat next to her. Soon, the owner sent hot ginger tea and a plate with a few glucose biscuits. A young boy placed the tray of tea on a small table kept there and left.

'It is so soothing to be back to the simple life.' she thought, looking at the clean cups and saucers kept next to a small tea kettle of steel, covered with a clean, white napkin. She poured some tea for herself and for Milind.

'A sensible size of the cup, a sensible portion,' she thought, remembering the cafes in the city, serving lukewarm coffee in the big cups. She handed over a cup of tea to Milind.

The backyards of all the neighbouring houses looked like a continuous stretch with hardly any wall or fencing marking their ownership. There was a whiff of burnt wood and a slight smoke rising up in the air, amid the greenery. This made Shubhangi remember her childhood. She got up from her chair, picked up her teacup and a biscuit. She walked a few steps and sat on a bench made of a plank cut out of a rock. She dunked her glucose biscuit in the tea and took a bite of the soft biscuit before sipping her tea. She relished the biscuit melting in her mouth but her mind wandered. She started thinking about her daughter, Manjari, while staring at the abstract texture of rough stone slab laid beneath her feet.

"First Manjari kept saying no to all the good alliances that came her way, now when she liked a couple of them, things are not moving forward," said Shubhangi to Milind.

She took another sip of tea and looked at her husband, who was engrossed in reading some article on his mobile. He did not respond.

"Tea is sweet. I will tell her to make it without sugar. But ginger is cutting the sweetness and giving a good taste." Shubhangi took one more sip and looked at Milind, who seemed oblivious to his surroundings, scrolling the screen of his phone, while holding his cup of tea in another hand.

"Kai tumhi! I am fed up with your mobile!! …. those days were better when you used to read the newspaper. At least I could snatch and throw that away." Shubhangi felt frustrated.

Milind looked at her and said, "Look around. It is beautiful. You wanted to come to this secluded place … why? Because your friend, Asavari had suggested! Now here too you are carrying the problems in your mind. Just forget everything and enjoy the surroundings."

He went back to his phone. His calm tone made Shubhangi feel more restless.

"First, you hold me responsible for everything then ask me to forget and enjoy. I know, you wanted to go to Goa." Shubhangi made a face then she wondered why she could not speak what she actually meant.

Milind bent his head, and looked at her with his eyebrows pulled up, his reading glasses slid down on his nose. He often did that, so he could go back to reading without removing and wearing the spectacles again.

"To tell you the truth, for me, any place is good. Yes, I would have preferred Goa over this terribly quiet place. And of course, sea-food and beer over your traditional vegetarian food but I am happy here too. I can be happy anywhere." He said, looked around and poured some more tea for himself and picked up the phone again.

Shubhangi fell silent. He was right. He could be happy anywhere.

'But he did not fail to mention, what he would have preferred, … so that I feel guilty for getting him here,' she thought.

'How come …' she often wondered, 'He has no expectations or things are actually happening his way? But then Manjari saying no to marriage is not what he wants. Is he doing anything to change Manjari's attitude? Nothing. Is it my responsibility alone ….?'

Shubhangi shook her head, as her head felt heavy. She got up and took a stroll in the backyard.

-::-

"You will love that place." Her friend Asavari had talked about Konkan enthusiastically. Seeing the photos of the place, Shubhangi had asked Milind to plan a trip to Konkan in the western ghats.

"Why don't you go with your friends?" Milind had suggested.

"All my life, I have been coming with you everywhere. Be it the weddings in the family or any other function. Why do I have to always coax you to make you come with me, where I want to go?" Shubhangi had asked.

She longed for his company. Milind mostly skipped family functions and travelled a lot because of his work. He did not know what to speak with the relatives or in social gatherings as all he could talk was about his work and financial investments.

He could not understand the emotional aspects of life and believed that raising children was Shubhangi's job and providing well, was his. Shubhangi had single handedly managed her growing children's problems and had helped them take decisions regarding their career and other issues in their life. Her children had seen their mother doing everything for them, listening to them, understanding and guiding them.

"Sometimes I need you Milind, to guide our children. I am not always enough. You are the one dealing with the world." Shubhangi would often tell him but at the same time she knew, Milind only knew two things. Do or don't do. Analysing, discussing the issues, were not his nature. Their children also preferred to speak with their mother.

-::-

"Papa, you must go. You must give company to Mom... now that we are away and have our own life to lead." Manjari had said.

"What life? Self-centred?" Milind had retorted.

Milind had not liked his daughter's condescending tone.

"Really papa? You are saying that? …..." Manjari was going to argue further but Shubhangi had gestured her to be quiet.

"Anyway, Papa, it would be a good change, if you both go together." Manjari had insisted before leaving for Hyderabad. She knew that her father was upset because she had turned down the suggested alliances. But Manjari did not like it when her father outrightly held her mother responsible for this. Eventually Shubhangi too started believing that it was her fault; even when her daughter was happy with her single status.

-::-

The backyard of each house had stretched up to the seashore. She saw the rows of coconut trees on both the sides of a narrow pathway. She had finished her tea. She got up and wrapped her stole around her shoulder and felt the morning breeze on her cheeks.

'It is not sultry here,' she thought and looked around. The backyard of their traditional Konkani homestay had a capsule shaped copper vessel with a dome shaped lid on the top. The vessel resembled the electric geyser with a pipe passing through the centre that would get heated with the firewood or coal kept on a grill at the bottom. The vessel was kept on a tripod, so that one could keep the bucket and could get the water from the tap attached to water heating vessel.

'I am seeing it after so long!' Shubhangi stood there, reminiscing the old days. She admired the carving of the brass tap and the handles on both the sides. There was a small opening on the dome shaped top cover. A tiny lid covered it. She was admiring the vessel, when she saw the homestay owner coming. The owner poured three buckets of water in the vessel and placed the dome shaped cover on the top. She kept the firewood and coal underneath the vessel.

She then opened the tiny lid and said,

"You can add the drops of bathing oil to it. But I add fresh Jasmin flowers. Once the water is hot, you can take out the water using the tap, but you will have to carry the bucket of hot water to the bathroom. I have not installed the electric geyser."

When Shubhangi mentioned that it was not possible for her to carry the bucket up the four steps nor for her husband, given his frozen shoulder.

"Don't worry, I will keep it or send my son." The lady said with a smile.

"You just ring the bell, but you must take bath while this lot of firewood is consumed." She pointed at the wood chunks and a tiny heap of coal kept beside.

Shubhangi had felt little uneasy as the owner was of her age but was so swift in running around. She was not slim like Shubhangi but looked healthy. She had clear and glowing complexion. Shubhangi found her beautiful, with her oiled hair tightly pulled back and tied in a bun, decked up with a string of jasmine flowers. A light green cotton saree with a matching blouse. Half a dozen green glass bangles, bordered with gold bangles in both the wrists and powdered bindi pressed on her forehead.

"You can have two to three buckets of hot water at one time and then we will refill it." She spoke in a tone like she meant it. Shubhangi understood, that just because they were paying, unnecessary wastage of fuel was not acceptable to her. She agreed to take bath early. She loved the smell of smoke infused with the smell of fresh Jasmine flowers in the water.

"I will serve fresh Poha, batata vada, coconut barfi and tea at eight thirty." Then looking at Shubhangi's face, she asked with a smile, "At nine-thirty?"

"Yes." Shubhangi said with a sigh.

She loved the smell of burning wood. Milind had overheard the conversation. He said, "I will take bath first."

Shubhangi understood that, as always, he would like to go out for his walk before the breakfast. He preferred to go alone. Shubhangi wished, they could do a few things together, at least sometimes if not every day. It was after a long time they were sitting together in the morning.

'Maybe I spoiled it by discussing children's marital status again.' She thought and sulked. She felt lonely.

"Ma. you have developed the habit of holding yourself responsible, for everything that goes wrong." Once Manjari had mentioned. Shubhangi shook her head and looked around.

A huge circular copper tub with round carved brass handles on the sides, was kept near a big stone slab, next to the copper water heater. It was apparent that people could take bath there in the open. On the left side, four chairs and a table were placed, on a slightly raised area that was covered with old stone tiles.

Milind was still having his tea there. After walking a few steps, she saw, a hammock was tied between two coconut trees. Trees were bent towards each other, as if wanting to kiss.

Shubhangi smiled and thought of lying in the hammock, but the narrow pathway towards the sea, allured her more than the hammock. She started walking towards the beach. She looked up and realised that there were many trees and the sky was hardly visible.

She was so upset with Milind that she decided to keep walking towards the sea shore without informing him. The sea at a distance appeared like a silver line, while she was walking through the avenue of trees, creepers, and shrubs. The whole green foliage made the surroundings little dark in the morning.

'It looks like cold sea shores as shown in the old English movies. Only blue and grey.' she thought and looked around but to her surprise she found herself alone and there were no shacks. Just a long stretch of deserted beach, with greenery behind her and sea in front.

She removed her foot wear and started walking towards the sea.

"Do not try to venture in the sea water. No matter how good a swimmer you may be. There are whirlpools in the sea, even near the shore. Those may pull you in. Many have lost their lives." She remembered her homestay owner's warning.

She stopped just where the sand was wet. She started walking on the beach, parallel to the sea. She felt like she was carrying a lot of weight on her shoulder. Her son, Shantanu had divorced just after three years of his marriage. It was a shock for both Shubhangi and Milind.

"How come children don't want to stay married? Why can't you tell them?" Milind would often get angry but he would never have a conversation with children.

"How can you force them to live together if they both don't wish? It is not like old times when women quietly compromised." Shubhangi would argue.

"Why? My mother was happy, you are happy. What compromises did you make?" Milind would ask.

'What presumptions!' She wanted to scream but Shubhangi could never give voice to those words. Often fight would shift to their own marriage ultimately, making the matter worse.

-::-

Shubhangi kept walking quietly but her mind was full of conflict.

'Where did I go wrong? Milind was never around when children were growing up. Yes, he was totally engrossed in his work, mostly on tours. But he could have tried to hear me out and understand me. He neglected me. Now he is holding me responsible for our son, Shantanu's divorce and for our daughter Manjari's decision to not get married.' Shubhangi stopped for a while with a forlorn look at the horizon.

'No sunrise at the horizon? Oh, how can it be? I am at the western shore.' She though and started walking again.

'Am I a western shore too? Sinking everything? Am I really responsible for the decisions that my children have made?', she could not walk further. Her head was spinning. She stopped, bent down and held her knees for a while before she sat down. The touch of sand on her hands made her feel good. She started running her finger in the sand making random designs. She then stretched her legs and flexed her feet. Her mind wandered again.

"You have poisoned her mind with your so-called feminist thoughts. Marriage is necessary for girls. Who will take care of her once we are gone?" Milind would get angry whenever Manjari would turn down a proposal.

"Has she not been living on her own for last so many years?" Shubhangi would ask him. "And I also want her to settle." She would keep switching between being a woman and being a mother.

"Ma, what is the meaning of getting settled? Getting married? Bhaiya got settled then they separated. What is the guarantee? I do not want all those hassles. I make money, I don't need a husband. I am happy." Once Manjari had said blatantly.

That had jolted Shubhangi. She had felt both humiliated and shocked. She felt, she had made herself so small in the eyes of her own daughter.

"Husband and money are synonyms? What about the companionship?" Shubhangi had asked her back.

"What companionship? Did you get any?" Manjari had thrown a rhetorical question.

Shubhangi had preferred to stay silent.

-::-

Shubhangi looked at the waves coming to the shore and returning with the same intensity. Her inner conflict was still on. Her mind was constantly struggling with the questions.

'Did we make marriage look so bad for our children? I think we did! Yes, we did. If Milind now wants his children to be married, he too should have worked to make this institute look good with his own involvement as an example.' She thought and looked at the horizon.

As she was thinking, she started swinging her arms with her palms on the sand. Impressions of many semi circles were created in the sand on both sides of herself. When she stopped, she noticed that, she was sitting in a circle made by her own hands, while her legs were outside of it.

'My feet are free to walk but my mind is not...., can I make my mind free?' She thought and looked up. She was so lost in her thoughts that she didn't realise that the sun had risen up in the sky. Soft morning rays were shining on the waves of the sea water. The sky at the horizon looked blue and clear; not misty and grey what it was some time ago.

Shubhangi smiled and she felt as if some weight was off her chest.

'My job is done. I am now free.' She told herself, got up and shook the sand from her track pants and t-shirt.

She started walking. The sea breeze felt cool on her face. She suddenly started walking fast, and felt a strong wave of happiness within her.

"I want to fly!!!" She shouted, and screamed..... she started running. She ran faster, she ran exuberantly, she felt infinite untapped energy within her, she did not think of anyone .... her eyes were welled up with the tears of joy, she started running fast, burst into laughter and kept running with her arms stretched out, her hair swaying, tears rolling down her cheeks ...

"Don't run into the sea ...there are whirlpools, that will pull you in .... bai ga!" A local woman wearing nine-yard saree and carrying a bundle of firewood on her head, waved at her and called out.

"Don't worry, tai! I know .... mala mahit aahe!" Shubhangi waved at her and exclaimed.

"I am now out of all the whirlpools..." She shouted at the top of her lungs. Shubhangi kept running, with both her arms stretched, outward.

The local woman smiled and started walking again.

Inheritance

"Madhu, did you read the paper today?"

Ajit climbed up the steps to veranda and asked his wife, who was sitting on a cane chair. Ajit had ordered a set of sofas, chairs and a table, made of cane from Siliguri to be kept in the veranda, that Madhu had decorated aesthetically. Earthen pots with different plants, were neatly arranged along the iron railing on the edge of the veranda. She loved watering the plants herself, while the gardener took care of the lawn.

Alongside the steps to Veranda, there was a pillar covered with the black granite, and a big cement planter was built connecting veranda and the pillar. Madhu had planted varieties of money plants in that planter. The creepers had spiralled up the black pillar. She made sure that each leaf was visible.

"Yes, I read. You are talking about Shilpa, right?", Madhu asked.

"Yes, Subodh's daughter has won the gold medal at the state level junior Badminton Championship," he said, while taking his shoes off. "We will go to Subodh's house after dinner to congratulate them. Have children had their dinner? We will take them along."

"Yes, girls had dinner. They are in their room, reading their books. I will tell them." Madhu said rearranging the magazines on the table.

Ajit got up and placed his shoes in the wooden shoe rack, kept in the foyer. The wooden shoe-rack had a marble top. Madhu had placed a beautiful vase on it and her daughters helped her arrange flowers every alternate day. She had kept a basket made with dry leaves to keep the knick-knacks. She had designed the rack herself and had got it made from a local carpenter. There was a comfortable chair kept next to it. She had placed her father-in-law's antique jacket stand alongside the shoe-rack.

Madhu was passionate about decorating home. Each corner of their Bungalow reflected her refined choice in carefully selected tapestry, furniture, paintings and crockery.

Both Ajit and Madhu loved entertaining people. Ajit had inherited this trait from his father who was a renowned and a successful lawyer. His father was the only one to have made it big in his generation in the family, so he had helped all his siblings financially for education and other needs. Ajit had inherited the same attitude, to be helpful towards his relatives. He was generous to anybody, who asked for help. He carried an unexplained sense of guilt for being the only one to be successful and wealthy among his cousins. Like his father, he too felt socially obligated to help others. Though he was ambitious and very hard working but he believed in sharing the success and the wealth and was inclusive by nature.

Ajit had not followed his father's footstep to become a lawyer. He was a mechanical engineer. He was running a successful business of manufacturing industrial machinery tools. Madhu had taken the charge of home and extended family, single handedly, that allowed Ajit to focus and grow in his business.

-::-

"Today I read the interview of Sonia Gandhi taken by Pushpa Bharti in 'Dharmyug' magazine. There is a series of interesting interviews. Like Amitabh Bachchan, Ravi Shastri! You know, Amitabh Bachchan and Rajeev Gandhi were childhood friends!" Madhu had developed a habit of telling whatever she could in such short moments of conversation. Ajit could not spend much time with his family being very busy in his profession.

After dinner, Ajit and Madhu along with their daughters, Megha and Anagha, headed to Subodh's place. On their way, they stopped to buy some sweets and a bouquet of flowers.

"Papa, let's buy some chocolates, Shilpa and her brother Shashank, they both love chocolates." Anagha, his elder daughter said.

"Sure, why not?" said Ajit with an encouraging approval.

Ajit parked the car in front of his cousin, Subodh's house. They received a warm welcome. Ajit and Madhu congratulated Subodh and his wife, blessed their daughter and wished her to achieve more success in the future. Anagha and Megha happily gave Shilpa the bouquet of flowers, and gift boxes of chocolates to both Shilpa and her brother Shashank.

Shilpa, Subodh's daughter, who had won the tournament, was the centre of attention. She enjoyed every moment of adulation being showered upon her. The conversation in the room mostly revolved around sports, and the routine Shilpa had to follow to maintain the fitness. Later, when Ajit got up to leave, Shilpa enthusiastically asked,

"Ajit Uncle, will you click my picture with your car? I will sit with my medal on the bonnet." Shilpa's parents fondly looked at her.

"Ok beta, but I have not brought my camera. Next time, we will." Ajit told his niece Shilpa.

"Promise, Uncle?" Shilpa was persistent. "Don't forget," she spoke in a little authoritative tone. She was beaming with confidence with her achievement and the admiration that followed.

Anagha felt little awkward. Both she and Megha were not used to speak in such tone with their parents. Demanding something from others was out of their imagination. When she saw Shilpa pestering her father, Anagha felt Shilpa was stepping into her world. Then she immediately felt guilty as they were taught to be sharing and be inclusive. She forced herself not to feel bad and told Shilpa,

"I will remind Papa to get the camera next time," she said but felt pretentious and could not understand the inner conflict.

"Yay!" Shilpa jumped with a joy.

"Promise. I will not forget." Ajit smiled, patted Shilpa's head. He then shook Subodh's hands and said, "If anything required, let me know. If you are required to be dropped or picked up at the railway station, while going for the next tournament, I will send my driver with the car."

He took Subodh aside, "Subodh, I know, coaching in sports is not easy. In case you need any financial help, let me know, Shilpa is like our daughter, just like Megha and Anagha."

"Thank you, Ajit." Subodh felt overwhelmed. "I will let you know."

Ajit and his family drove back home. Megha was half asleep and Anagha was quiet. Madhu could not understand why there was an awkward silence. Usually, their daughters would be talking nonstop.

"Camera is in the office. Remind me to bring it home tomorrow." Ajit told Madhu. He used camera for taking photos in manufacturing units.

"Papa, you never praise us, like Subodh Uncle was praising Shilpa." Anagha said after a while in a little hesitant tone.

Anagha and Megha were not very close to him, because of his busy schedule. Madhu who was managing them both with their school, studies, and health. She would also be busy managing home, relatives and guests. Ajit sometimes used to invite his friends and their families, from his business circle, for dinner at home and Madhu would look after that too.

Ajit smiled and looked back, "Beta, we love you. It is when the world praises you, that is the real achievement."

Anagha was twelve-year-old and was convinced. 'We are a family; we anyway love each other.' Anagha thought.

"Papa, I will click Shilpa's pictures." Megha, who was eight-year-old, suddenly woke up and spoke with enthusiasm. She somehow wanted to use the camera.

"Good girl." Ajit said.

"No, you are not old enough. Isn't it Papa?" Anagha asked Ajit for validation.

Madhu turned back and said, "Both of you can click the photos."

Megha clapped and teased Anagha.

"Ok." Anagha accepted silently. She wanted to question that why was she made to wait these many years and Megha gets to operate the camera so early? But she knew such protests would make her look small. And she was supposed to be the mature one.

Ajit looked at Madhu, "It is good to feel happy for the achievement of others. I want to teach them to be inclusive."

Madhu agreed, as Ajit was genuinely inclusive. He would be equally involved in welcoming Madhu's siblings and their children too. Madhu also devoted herself for the extended families of both the sides.

-::-

Madhu's sister and brother visited during the holidays. Ajit and Madhu were enthusiastic to make different plans for them.

Ajit also offered on job training to Anagha's college going twin cousins.

"It will certainly help you when you step out in the real world for work."

"Ajit Uncle is great." Madhu's nephews had said unanimously.

"Why don't you learn driving as well?" He asked them, "You both are eighteen. I will send my driver."

Madhu was baking a cake for everyone. She then asked her sister, "Didi, what should we make for dinner? Other than Jijaji's favourite matar-paneer, that I have already planned. What else?"

"Masi....Malai-Koftas!", "Bua,...Matar-kachori!" Children demanded and Madhu happily fulfilled everybody's wish during their stay. Sometimes Ajit would return home late but would make sure to take guests out for ice cream, post dinner.

Anagha had started feeling something odd with people visiting and praising her parents, Madhu and Ajit so much. She felt, her aunts and uncles did not behave in the same manner the way her parents did.

"Why everyone feels so happy in our house but we don't feel the same when we go to somebody's house?" She often wondered.

Anagha and her cousins were ready to go out with their mothers, when Ajit called Anagha and gave her an envelope, "Give this to Mummy."

Anagha went in and gave it to her mother, who was getting ready to go for shopping with her sister and sister-in-law. Ajit would make it sure that the guests were given proper gifts and he had given that responsibility to Madhu.

"Anagha, keep this envelope in my purse, we will go to Subodh Uncle's house first, to give this to him. These are Shilpa's photographs." Madhu told Anagha, while pinning up the pallu of her Saree.

"I am ready, too." Madhu's elder sister, Lata entered the room, looking happy and fresh. For everyone, visiting Madhu's house was like staying in a hotel, with no work to do and having enough rest in the privacy of the guestroom.

Anagha kept the envelope in her mother's purse. She felt tempted to open and see Shilpa's photographs. 'It is open, not pasted. I can see, I am not doing anything wrong.', twelve-year-old Anagha assured herself and opened the envelope. She saw five glossy photographs of her cousin Shilpa, sitting on the bonnet of the car with the gold-medal around her neck. Another one was with her parents. Then there was one with she holding the steering wheel of the car. Anagha first smiled seeing the pictures of her cousin and was awestruck with the way she was sitting in the car, with one hand on the steering and holding medal with the other one.

'Even I don't have such photos in our car! Can I ever be like her? Will anyone do such special things for me? Will my photo also be published in the newspaper?', Anagha thought. She kept the photos back in the envelope. She placed the envelope in her mother's purse and had a feeling that she could not explain to her mother.

Anagha and her cousin sat in the front seat of the car, while her mother and aunts sat behind. One of her aunts, looking at her mother's Saree, said, "Your Saree is beautiful, must be very expensive."

Madhu smiled, "Yes, such expensive ones, even I don't buy, this one was gifted."

Anagha heard and found it strange, 'Why is mummy lying?'

She knew her mother often bought sarees of floral prints. She had heard words like Georgette and Chiffon from her mother. Anagha loved how her mother looked so beautiful in such sarees. Madhu and Ajit often underplayed their status. It was their effort to be one with everybody around. Eventually Anagha too learned the same. She felt guilty for having expensive dresses or toys for herself.

Later Anagha saw her mother gifting similar sarees to her Masi, Mami and Bua. Madhu had also bought gifts for their children. Anagha saw happy and smiling faces of her cousins and their parents and her own parents as well. Anagha felt happy but also sensed some conflict creating in her mind that she could not understand.

-::-

Ajit's business was growing manifolds. He would even offer financial help to anybody in need and people would accept without any hesitation. Once Anagha heard her mother telling her father,

"Don't lend money for buying plots. They should not buy, if they don't have money. Our daughters are growing, we will need money for their education." Madhu sounded worried.

Ajit had blind trust in his friends and relatives. "They will return." He assured Madhu. They seldom did, Instead, some of them would advise him adversely.

"Ajit, you can accumulate more wealth, if you stop showing your income so honestly and avoid paying so much tax." Once a relative suggested.

"And lose my sleep and health as well." Ajit had replied with a smile. "No. I believe in honesty and that keeps me going."

Anagha felt proud of her father and she dreamed of becoming like him.

-::-

Anagha was fourteen and Megha was ten when their parents planned a trip to southern India. Anagha was praying for everything to go smooth. Their last trip to Rajasthan was cancelled as Prime Minister Indira Gandhi was assassinated and riots had erupted. Ajit could manage to get some time after long since then. Anagha and Megha were very excited. They were sitting with their parents.

"I will book the air tickets both ways this time, so that we could spend more time in sight seeing." Madhu and her daughters were happy as they were going out together after a long time. Ajit was checking his passbook and was writing his chequebooks at night.

"Tomorrow, I will go to the bank and then to Air India office. Madhu, keep this cash for shopping and other expenditures during the trip." He said and handed over some cash to Madhu.

"I already have a list of silk sarees, sandalwood artefacts that our relatives have asked for." Madhu said, keeping the cash in a bag.

"Nobody brings anything for us." Anagha blurted out.

"We don't gift people in expectation of any return, we gift to them because we love them." Madhu had explained.

"So, that means nobody loves us?" Anagha was a teenager and had acquired an argumentative trait. Madhu often found her right but never had answers to her questions. Just then the phone rang.

"At this time?" Madhu wondered.

Ajit went to the living room to pick up the phone and reacted in a worrisome tone. He returned to the room, where everybody was sitting.

"It was my cousin, Milind. His son is admitted in the hospital. He needs money urgently. Also, there has to be someone with him."

"Oh, what happened? How will you send money? Madhu asked.

"I will drive to him. It is just a four-hour drive." Ajit said without losing a moment. "Give me the money that I just gave you. I have signed the cheque. Tomorrow, you go to the bank and withdraw more."

Madhu immediately took out the envelope and handed him over.

"Are you sure, you are going to drive at this hour? What if you go in the morning?" Madhu asked with concern.

"Madhu, it is urgent! How could you even think anything else?" Ajit said.

"I will call Raju; he will accompany me. Don't worry." Ajit said to assure Madhu, though he knew, his assistant Raju was on leave.

Madhu immediately packed his overnight bag, just in case he had to spend a day. Their trip to south India did happen but Madhu and Ajit curtailed on their own shopping while things promised to relatives were bought.

Anagha by then had understood that unlike others, their family was not about just four of them but it was about everybody they knew.

It was not always about helping people financially, Anagha saw her parents working in the weddings in the extended family, attending people in the hospital, sending them tiffin. She saw her parents loving everyone around them.

Anagha had inherited the same qualities, though she objected when she sensed that her parents were being taken for granted. Meanwhile her younger sister Megha, had learned to be self-centred.

Ajit and Madhu offered the help before one could ask. Once an old aunt of Ajit came and stayed with them for six months to recuperate from her illness. She recovered and went back to her home. She tried to pay Ajit for the medical expenses but he refused to take it. That was the day when Anagha witnessed a heated argument between her mother and father.

"That is not right, Ajit. Let her pay for her own medical expenses. She has enough money to look after herself." Madhu was upset.

"Madhu, we can make more money, but accepting money from her for the medical expense will make your invaluable dedication look so small. Understand that." Ajit tried to explain Madhu.

Anagha heard this conversation and was confused that, who was right?

-::-

Anagha passed out from National Institute of Designing, Ahmadabad and joined a big firm in Mumbai. Eventually, she got married and started her own firm. Megha, went abroad to study on a full scholarship, met her life partner there, got married and settled in the USA.

Anagha noticed, most of their relatives were not there to celebrate her and Megha's success. Some chose not acknowledge. When she mentioned it to her younger sister, Megha; she seemed least bothered, "They don't picture in my life. I don't involve myself with them."

Anagha was a sensitive person, she would easily develop a bond with people. Megha had moved away while Anagha continued living life the way her parents lived.

-::-

Years passed by. Anagha's children were in college. One day she woke up to a call early in the morning. It was her father.

"Oh my God! How did it happen? he was fine. Just last month, Subodh Uncle and Sandhya Aunty had returned from London after visiting their daughter, Shilpa and son Shashank. They both had stayed at my place." Anagha was shocked to learn about the death of Subodh Uncle.

"How is Sandhya aunty managing? Shilpa and Shashank must be devastated." Anagha was concerned.

"Anagha, you mother is with her. We do not know, how long Shilpa and Shashank will take to reach India.", we are still in the hospital.

"Papa, don't worry, I am reaching there as soon as possible.", Anagha said and disconnected the call.

Madhu and Ajit had made arrangements for the last rights, while her cousins were yet to reach from London. Anagha reached before them and helped her parents. A week after the funeral, everybody came to stay in Ajit and Madhu's house. Anagha was feeling bad for her cousins Shilpa and Shashank.

"Ma, I cannot stay longer." Shilpa told her mother.

"Let us sort out property issues before that." Shashank was little upset.

"Ajit Uncle, I have to go back. I cannot stay further. All these official formalities of getting the documents made, sorting mother's pension related issues, is going to take too long."

Ajit and Madhu offered to help and assured Shashank and Shilpa not to worry. Anagha thought her cousins would be thankful to her parents. Instead, they completely handed over their mother's responsibility to Ajit and Madhu.

"I think it would be nice, if you extend your stay in India and complete all the formalities." Anagha suggested her cousins.

"But Ajit Uncle said, we can go back now. He will manage everything. Also, my mom feels close to your mom. So, she will stay with them for a few months till we come again. ….. and you know it, who can say no to Ajit Uncle? I need to respect that." Anagha's cousin Shashank said.

Anagha smiled, she knew, this was how it was meant to be. She made tea for everyone and decided to extend her stay to lighten up the load that her parents had now. She looked at Shilpa who was packing her bags and then she looked at the grief-stricken face of Shilpa's mother, who was once so proud of her daughter.

'And I wanted to be like her…!' Anagha could not help reminisce her childhood memory.

-::-

Ajit had wound up his business. He had made sure all his employees got a good job elsewhere. He was now working freelance as a consultant.

Both Madhu and Ajit were living a quiet life in their bungalow that was still telling the story of its grand past, with the hustle and bustle and a peaceful present, at the same time. Veranda, that used to be occupied with guests, and witnessed many conversations over tea, still looked vibrant with plants and the evening breeze.

Kitchen, that used to be filled with the aroma of variety of meals being cooked from morning till evening, for a gathering of extended family, up on the terrace at night in summers or in the backyard of the bungalow in the winters, around a bonfire; was still active to dish out the favourite food to the guest. Their house was a home for all, embracing every visitor with love and care.

Now, there were no relatives and friends visiting them, who used to be fond of Ajit and Madhu.

Anagha would visit them more often now as she could manage her firm online. During one such visits Madhu and Anagha were having their tea, sitting in the veranda. Madhu was looking at her money plant, she had sprayed the water on the leaves making them shine. She took a few sips of tea and stared at the money plant spiralling around the black granite pillar.

"We have always been surrounded with so many people, for years. Life just passed by." Madhu said.

"Ma, do you really think that all those people whom you and Papa helped, made them part of your family with your love and concern, also had the same feelings for us?" Anagha looked at her with a question in her eyes.

"Why do you ask so?" Madhu asked Anagha in a soft tone.

"I don't know," said Anagha.

"I know, what you mean. I never gave it a thought. We lived our life the way we knew. ... it felt good to have people around, it felt good to be useful to others. We liked it and we still do." Madhu said with a smile.

Anagha felt guilty for disturbing her mother's perfectly peaceful perceptions of life.

"I don't know, how to tell you..." Anagha said.

"Aren't you and Megha doing the same?" Madhu asked.

'It is not the same anymore, in fact it probably never was ... relationships were need based.' Anagha wanted to say but she just smiled and nodded.

"Good then," Madhu looked at the clock on the wall, "It is time for my walk now. Mrs. Reddy must be waiting for me in the park."

She then looked at Anagha and said, "See, what wrong has happened to us? We are happy, and at peace." Anagha agreed. She waved bye to her mother and waited for her father to return from his walk.

Ajit came home from his usual one hour walk and asked Anagha if she would like to have coffee. He enjoyed making coffee for his family and have some talk.

Anagha too loved having coffee and conversation with her father, whenever she visited her parents. She took pride in him being self-reliant. Though she could not stop him from going out of the way to help others, given his age, but had accepted, that is what he was.

Ajit was happy that next month his younger daughter, Megha was coming. He was watching the milk to boil when he heard Anagha speaking to someone on the phone,

"Yes, hotel will be a better option."

Later, Anagha told Ajit that she had received a call from a relative.

"Papa, she was asking if I would be back home by next weekend, if not, then she would book a hotel. She, along with her family is in transit and has a stopover in Mumbai, so she needs a place to stay for a couple of days."

Anagha then looked at her father, "I told her, I will not be home and she can go ahead with booking a hotel."

"But you will be there," said Ajit handing over a cup of coffee to her.

"Papa, last time, she had dropped her old mother at my place for a month, so that she could go for a trip. I took very good care of her mother, now it has become a practice. Our house is just like a hotel for them. There is no bonding or sense of attachment … It all feels one way. I invest emotionally, mentally, physically …I invest my time… my children know sharing …. But something is missing and is painful. And it is not just about any one person… with most it is like that …who wants bonding and love? Services can be bought in the market." Anagha was restless. She knew, her father would not understand.

"It is your call, but are you feeling better?" Ajit asked.

"No, actually I am not! Honestly …. how can one unlearn to love, to be concerned, … how can one help without emotions? Emotions, that are simply being used, I feel cheated." Anagha took a sip and wondered how her parents never felt the way she did. 'Did I miss on inheriting some gene?' She smiled at her own thought.

"Anagha, if you are able to help others, isn't it a good thing? You are the blessed one." Ajit said.

"Yes Papa," Anagha said. "But sometimes we have to help ourselves too."

Ajit knew, it was for her to decide. He smiled at her and then looked outside. The sky reflected the orange hues of the sun that was setting.

www.ingramcontent.com/pod-product-compliance
Lightning Source LLC
LaVergne TN
LVHW061615070526
838199LV00078B/7297